A Patriot Peacemaker

The Story of Seth,

A Tale from Walloon Lake

—✦—

Novel by
Dennis Schall Brogan
The Sustainable Press

Copyright © 2023 Dennis Schall Brogan

All rights reserved. This book or any portion thereof may not be reproduced or used in any manner whatsoever without the express written permission of the publisher except for the use of brief quotations in a book review.

ISBN: 979-8-9860113-3-2 (paperback)
ISBN: 979-8-896-0113-4-9 (eBook)

The Sustainable Press
207 Hancock Drive Syracuse
New York 13207

Dedication

This book is dedicated to the citizens of the Onondaga Nation for their stewardship of the Earth and wisdom. To Grace Hall Hemingway, her creative spirit engulfs Walloon Lake, MI. This book is dedicated to Grace Hemingway's great-great-granddaughter Cristen Hemingway Jaynes who inspired me to tell stories.

Writing is honesty- Matthew Espo

Book Disclaimer

The story, all names, characters, and incidents portrayed in this book are fictitious. No identification with actual persons (living or deceased), places, buildings, and products is intended or should be inferred.

The Story of Seth

It was a crisp sunny April morning as the bugler played taps. Archie Myers Andersson would have been ninety-two years old today. Seth, Archie's grandson stood at attention as the Marine Corps Guard handed him the flag which had been draped on Archie's casket. Seth, like his grandfather had been a Marine too, serving his nation. Archie was laid to rest in St. Clement Catholic Cemetery across the road from the end of the runway of Pellston Airport. Archie had been a Marine Pilot who flew missions after World War II. It was fitting the old man would hear the planes and jets take off and land flying by his grave.

Semper Fi, Seth thought as the flag touched his fingertips one lone tear slid from the edge of his right eye.

Damn it, he thought, he did not cry much. However, the sorrows of losing his Grand Pop had broken down his six-foot eight-inch frame. And then an emotion of joy swept through him.

Semper Fi old man, Semper Fi …

An hour later the family, patrons and what few friends left of Archie's were gathered at Andersson's Pub located just south of Mackinaw City, Michigan on US Route 31. Better known as Archie's Place. Seth owned it now and like his grandfather he was born to be a publican. As much as the day was a celebration of Archie's life there was also a very special celebration about to take place.

Seth's wife Betsy was pregnant, well not really just pregnant, she was due today, tomorrow or the next day to bring their first child into the world. John Ernest Longfield would be his name. And the little boy would grow up in Indian River, Michigan where Archie had taught Seth to hunt and fish and to love the depth of nature in the land of Nick Adams. Archie had been a Hemingway fan and knew some of the Hemingway's who still summered at Walloon Lake. Seth honored the family lore by giving John the middle name Ernest.

Seth looked out at the crowd gathered and saw Betsy.

God, he thought to himself. She is more beautiful today than the day we danced at the Mackinaw Apple Butter Festival when they were both fifteen.

He looked beyond where Betsy was holding court with the other young mothers and saw Niles.

The old friend of Archie's was sitting in his normal spot which was always the second stool from the end. Niles and Archie were fishing buddies, hunting buddies, drinking buddies and most of all best friends. Brothers from another mother they would laugh as each told jokes and stories that could fill the Chicago Tribune. Niles was Seth's godfather.

Seth worked his way behind the three busy bartenders. He laughed inside himself, free drinks for everyone, an open bar. God how Archie hated to buy anyone a drink he thought. Well, the old barkeep was buying them today. Seth reached up over the bar to a cupboard and slid the key in the latch he had removed from around his neck. It had been around Archie's until the day he died. Now it was Seth's key to hold.

The old man had told his grandson that after his services and everyone was enjoying the moment at the bar, he was to gather Archie's friends in attendance and open the door on the cabinet. There would be a note inside with a bottle. Seth eased the key in the latch and giggled it to the left. Nope, he thought, it's a right turn lock. A few pieces of dust fluttered down into his eyes.

He lifted the little box inside the cupboard down and walked over to Niles. The old man looked up at Seth, his eyes were glassy from crying.

Niles reached over and put his arm on Seth's right forearm. "I miss him so bad Seth."

So did Seth but he had to be strong for Niles and everyone here today. "Gramps left a note for you and I and any of his friends. I would assume in the box is a bottle of some pretty fine spirits."

Seth handed the letter over to Niles and asked him to read it. Niles took a moment and then with his left hand shaking lightly grasped the small piece of paper. He opened it and laughed out loud…

Seth, wondering what the hell was so funny took the paper from Niles. His deep dark laugh filled the front half of the barroom. Niles read it again.

"Screw you boys, this is the last drink I will ever buy you. Be Well and God Bless AMA."

The AMA stood for Archibald Meyers Andersson.

Seth took the little key taped to the top of the box and handed it to Niles who gingerly opened the old wood box. Inside was a truly old bottle of Jaquin's Grande Reserve Napoléon French Brandy that had to be fifty or more years old. And it had never been opened.

Niles handed the bottle across the mahogany wood bar. Seth inspected the bottle and held it up to the small light by the end of the bar. Damn, the bottle was still full. He grabbed two brandy style sipping glasses and broke the seal on the bottle. Both men could smell the sweet, distilled aroma wafting up from the bottle. Seth poured two generous glasses of this reddish blue hued liqueur. It was time for a toast. Niles held the glass beneath his nostrils and breathed in the fumes of the old brandy. Seth followed his actions. WOOOH the brandy gave both men a little nasal buzz.

Niles looked at the lumbering giant of a man that Seth represented and gave a toast.

"To a god damn good man who knew that the greatest strength is being kind to all and making a difference every day. To Archie my brother and friend. Peace, Love, Sunshine."

They both slowly touched their lips to the glass and took a sip.

MMMMMMMMMM, that was good and without thinking both threw the remaining brandy down the Ole' Hatch as Archie would state when they were drinking at the hunting cabin. Seth raised the bottle and poured two more glasses. Another toast and another. It would not take long before the bottle was empty, and the memories of Archie filled the stories told by both men at the end of the bar. Sometimes wisdom does not come in the bottle sometimes it arrives after the bottle is consumed thought Seth.

Semper Fi Old Man, Semper Fi.

Ice and The Old Man

It had been a great winter out on the ice thought the old man. The ice was a solid thirteen inches thick of frozen lake below Niles Gunderson's feet. He had fished these waters for some eighty-four years, spring, summer, winter and fall. Niles grandfather had pulled the ice sled with the little boy sitting tall out on the ice when he was just four years old. Those moments were still fresh in the old man's memory.

The wind had come up a little bit since he trudged out on the ice to one of his favorite fishing spots. It was a small cove that had a long rock type reef which ran out some one hundred yards from the point on the west edge of the cove. Niles had filled his bucket with the legal limit of fresh lake perch and one incredible Walloon Lake walleye.

The sun was beaming down on this late Tuesday morning as Niles sat on his fishing stool. He leaned back and closed his eyes, letting the suns winter warmth shine down on his face. It was not June's sunny warmth showering him with sunlight, although for early March he could feel spring and summer edging out the cold of this winter.

Time to pack it in and head back to the cabin along the lakeshore for some lunch and then his afternoon nap. A good nap was always healthy, his mother Jenny had told him when he was five years old. Niles chuckled thinking of her stories, her beauty and her grace. He was blessed.

The old fisherman stood up and felt the pain in his upper chest. For the last six years he had taken medicine for angina that calmed the pain. He was a healthy old guy who could walk the ass off a mule he joked during deer hunting season here in Northern Michigan. The angina had started to occur more often lately, giving him more moments of difficulty breathing when they happened.

He rubbed his upper left chest as if to massage out the pain. Another deep breath, and another. It was getting hard to get air into his lungs and his pain grew as he started sweating. Damn, he thought, is this the… Down on the ice Niles tumbled, a slow slouching motion as he laid down in the soft snow from last night. He was down, the pain was so intense it felt like an ice pick was poking inside his chest. "Oh god", he whispered, "I hope someone finds me before the ice melts." And then the world went dark.

The lake had winter residents, however only a few would be out on the ice fishing today. Unless someone noticed Niles, he would either be dead from a heart attack or from hypothermia.

His mind was still engaged as he thought about all his friends before him and his wife Debbie who had passed away three years earlier. Would she be there in heaven to meet him? Christ would he even get to heaven? What if heaven does not exist and you just die. No seeing Debbie or his parents. No pearly gates or harps playing. Just darkness forever and that scared him more than anything.

He drifted further into what felt like freedom. Is this what it feels like when you die, he thought again Niles felt the chill of the ice begin to transfer from the snow and ice through his old wool coat. He had a feeling or thought as his mind raced and he could see his soul rising above him, hovering. Damn cold was the feeling. It must be cold in heaven and hot in hell, he smiled, his eyes still closed.

And then he felt it. A moist wetness across his face and forehead. Once, now twice, now three times. It shook Niles awake. His eyes opened to the suns glow, and he felt the warmth again. Then more wetness. Niles rolled to his right and saw Dusty, his trusty black lab retriever. Who in a dog's life was older than Niles licking his face. Damn dog, he chuckled as Dusty rolled in the snow next to him.

The old man was alive. He sat up and then stood brushing the snow off his pants and his jacket. Then grabbing the bucket and sled he trudged back across the ice following Dusty back to the cabin for a bowl of soup and a nap. Life on the lake was good he thought. Life was good and thank goodness for dogs and their companionship.

Native Sons

They were sons from another mother, blood brothers in the truest sense. Seth and John Owltree had served two tours in Afghanistan, had endured the wraths of war. John had Seth's six and Seth had John's. They were truly blood brothers as each had sustained grazing shoulder wounds several days apart. Seth had tended to Big Jake's shoulder and Jake had patched Seth arm which had a huge gash on his left arm from a piece of shrapnel. The shrapnel was from a roadside bomb that went off as a truck was going by a place Jake and Seth were posted at that one day.

John Oscar Owltree was a Native American, a member of the Wolf Clan of the Onondaga Nation south of Syracuse, NY. His mother was the Clan Mother of the Wolf Clan at Onondaga, his Uncle Orlin was a peace chief. Orlin Owltree had been a chief of the Nation and the Grand Council of the Haudenosaunee a long time. Seth had met the man once in Onondaga. Jake had brought his friend to the Onondaga Longhouse to meet the chiefs when they returned the last time from war.

After both had been discharged on the same day, the boys rented a GMC Yukon and toured US 1 from Key West to Boston exploring and attempting to leave the scars and brutality of the battles fought on the road behind them. The adventure had been fun and both men felt cleansed of that black ass feeling of war.

Seth had stayed two nights in the family cabin just up the hill above the Longhouse. Mrs. Owltree, Aubrey, she told to Seth to call her had filled the two warrior's bellies with Corn Chowder, fresh Venison, strawberries from the family garden. She made the best damn pancakes out of this stone-ground mix that were to die for. Covered in fresh warmed maple syrup. She had fattened the hogs as they say. Big Jake's spirit creature was the bear. And he looked the part. He was six foot eight inches tall like Seth, but more sleek and trim. And the boy could run…

Seth, like all Marine's at boot had to run every day. Sometimes in shorts and a tee shirt and sometimes with a full dress and pack loaded with stones. It did not matter stones or shorts; Big Jake was always first. The man could run like a buck during the rut.

Aubrey on the second night at the cabin around the fireplace and hearth had looked at Seth and laughed. She spoke softly, Seth listened and the Clan Mother asked, "What month were you born Seth?"

"May Mrs. Owltree. May 18th."

She smiled and laughed. The woman was a lady with immense power and grace thought Seth. She walked over to the mantle above the hearth and handed Seth the old powder bulls horn. He held it and felt something envelop his body. And Mrs. Owltree spoke. The horn still had powder in it.

"So, this was my great-great grandfather's powder horn. He carried it in the American Revolution when the Six Nations and colonialist fought the damn Brits." He held it, his hands feeling the power or the energy it contained. "Your name here in Onondaga and across the Six Nations of the Iroquois as your people call us will be one of great stature. For we do not pick our spirit animals lightly son."

Seth puzzled spoke, "what will I be called mother?" he blurted without thinking.

"I, we will call you Bull. It's you sign son. And your big enough to take on a country bull and win." The lady of the cabin laughed, and all followed in her joy. She had a new son from another mother and the nation had another warrior.

The next morning, they were told to put on their Marine Dress Uniform's, Full Dress as if they were meeting the president of the United States. And in this land, they were.

Both men fell asleep in the loft Jake had grown to miss when he was not on the nation. They awoke to the smell of venison summer sausage and bacon. After a full breakfast they showered outside in the exterior shower. Warm fresh water, and the chill of the morning still hanging in the air.

They pulled their uniforms from the closet to iron and press them as every Marine would do on a morning like this. To their amazement both uniforms were spit tight pressed with creases that could cut butter. They looked at each other and did not have to say anything. These two had this unique ability to look at the other and know what the other was thinking.

They dressed. Even their boots were spit polished.

The Clan Mother and her daughters had pressed the warriors' threads while they both slept. Outside the cabin members of the Onondaga Wolf Clan had assembled. The Clan was present to meet the warriors officially in the Onondaga tradition to walk with them to the Longhouse to be greeted by the Onondaga Chiefs.

The members all dressed in their best traditional style's. Two young boys led the procession throwing a lacrosse ball back and forth with the hand-crafted wooden stick each was given at birth.

It was not Fifth Avenue in New York City, no ticker tape, however Seth felt honored in a manner he had never experienced. As they arrived Seth saw the chiefs. Each had a headdress and wore traditional garb to.

When they were at war in Afghanistan Jake every morning recited the Thanksgiving Address, he was taught. In his native language. Seth always sat with his head bowed, praying himself. Over the months the two bonded, Seth had learned some of the Haudenosaunee language. He was not anywhere near proficient, but he understood Jake's words.

Mrs. Owltree introduced the two warriors to the

Tadodaho, Chief Carl Elm. An offering of tobacco was lit before the boys and the old chief began the Thanksgiving Address. When he did the two Marine's snapped to attention. It was almost twenty minutes before Chief Elm finished and walked up and gave his nephew a hug and then, he hugged Seth. Marines at ease now.

The two men followed the Onondaga Chiefs into the Longhouse. Besides the Onondaga Chiefs there were representatives from the Mohawk, Oneida, Cayuga, Seneca, Tuscarora and from across the Great Turtle Island as the native people called North America.

Jake had told Seth how this would go down. Enter and stand at attention until the chiefs sit. Then sit down and listen. When it was your time to talk someone would hand you an eagle feather. Jake sat, Seth stood nervously and then relaxed as the Tadodaho told a story about strength. The Tadodaho was the supreme leader of the Haudenosaunee.

It was a good story of how a man's strength is built to hunt for food, to build the longhouse and defend the nation. The chief was standing. When you spoke in the Longhouse you stood.

And then the chief spoke with a soft voice. "Boy's

you have been to war, you have witnessed the death of comrades, children and mothers. But I want you both to remember one thing. The greatest strength is gentleness."

Chief Elm sat down and handed the feather to his left. Each chief spoke, one after another. Stories from the past, from the French and Indian Wars to the American Revolution, War of 1812, the Civil War, World War I, World War II, Korea, and Vietnam. And now Afghanistan and Iraq. Blood had been spilled on Mother Earth and now was the time to heal.

The Onondagas, like all the Six Nations had fought alongside the Colonists in every war since the Revolution.

Soon the feather was handed to Seth. He stood at attention for a moment, saluted the chiefs while his body shook.

His mouth was dry, but he wet his lips and spoke.

"I want to give thanks to you and the people of Onondaga, to the citizens of the Six Nations for welcoming me home. Tomorrow, I go to Indian River, Michigan where my people and family live. I hope and pray that I am welcomed home as warmly and wonderfully as I have been here in my time at Onondaga. Today I stand here on the sovereign soil of the Onondaga Nation, tomorrow I will stand on my land. Jake is my brother, I mean John. One night out on patrol we were pinned down while some knuckle head morons peppered our little ditch with machine guns. Jake and I called into the base to one of our squad members and Jake spoke in your language. He taught us phrases and words the enemy would never understand. A minute later a rocket blew up that nest of death. We made a pact in the ditch that night. If his people or mine ever needed defending or a warrior each would be there for the other. He is my brother and if you ever need a six-foot eight ex-Marine you just call. I will come stand a post. I will stand guard on the wall."

Seth bowed his head left and then right and then to the Tadodaho.

The Old Chief stood. He motioned Seth to step forward. Sheepishly after a nod from Jake he stepped to the center of the longhouse and the leader put his hand on Seth shoulder. In the other he had a leather braided strap with an owl and turkey feather woven into the leather. Seth handed him the talking feather.

He spoke, first in the native tongue of the Onondaga. Then in English for Seth to understand the moment.

"Today our nation brings into the clans a new son, a son from another mother. Today the Bull becomes a citizen to our nation. You will be welcome on the Onondaga Nation and any native lands on Great Turtle Island as a member of the Onondaga Nation." He was not a member of one particular clan. He was a special human and a member of every clan of the Onondaga Nation. The old chief handed Jake the feathers tightly woven into the leather headdress.

Jake stood and told Seth to stay where he was as he told stories of the two warriors to the chiefs assembled. The chiefs consisted of war chiefs and peace chiefs. There were two men that had a special title of Faithkeepers. Like a rabbi or minister they were the preachers here. When all had spoken the assembly of native leaders listened as Chief Elm once more recited the Thanksgiving Address.

Seth was standing at attention with Jake as the wise ole' Indian spoke. The meeting was over, and it was time for the nation to celebrate the boy's return.

Come to Papa

The proud new father held his baby boy in his big mitts. Seth had the hands of a bear. They were strong hands and yet as he held the newborn boy, the softness of the new child's skin brought a tear to Seth's eye. In the last week he had cried as taps was played at his grandfather Archie's grave and now with the birth of his first son.

He looked at his princess, Betsy, who was gathering herself after four hours of birthing her first child. John Ernest Longfield was moments old as Seth told him his name, his heritage and the dreams he had for the boy. Where the tears earlier in the week had been tears of sorrow and loss, the tears streaming down the father's face were now tears of pure joy.

Seth was a faithful man just not a church going lad.

Betsy who was Catholic always joked to her friends at St. Clements Catholic Church that Seth was a Progressive Druid because he felt closer to God in the woods, fishing on the lakes around Indian River, Michigan, golfing with his buddies Sunday mornings or sitting in a tree stand in the fall.

He said a prayer, or rather spoke to his grandfather. "Pops, bless this boy with your wisdom and grace, keep him safe from all harm and worry. Teach him to be the best man he can be without the knowledge of being taught. And tell gramma that she should teach him to sing and love art," like she had done for him. Archie and Alva Andersson were Seth's grandparents. Seth's father Jackson had died when Seth was four. Archie and Alva were second parents to Seth and his sister when his mom worked weekends and nights at the Mackinaw Hospital. Archie taught the laws of nature and life while Alva taught him to read, draw, sing and play the piano. She taught his sister too.

Alva was from Madrid, Spain. Well, that's where she was born. Alva Ortiz was a nineteen-year-old sophomore at U of M, the University of Michigan, in Ann Arbor when the twenty-eight-year-old former Marine walked through the cafeteria for lunch. She was sitting at table alongside her friend Casey when he saw her. It was the smile that caught his attention. A smile that radiated across a room like the bright brilliant sunshine rising in the eastern morning sky.

Courage, he thought. Be witty and gentle.

Archie walked over and introduced himself and asked if he might join the two young women. "Hi, my name is Arch, mind if I sit with you ladies and enjoy some lunch?"

Casey looked up at the giant of a man and said "Sure, I'm Casey and this is my friend Alva." Casey was chatty and fired up the conversation. Like a wagon master holding the reins with a team of horses wanting to run, Archie held back his desire to speak as the red-haired schoolgirl from the Upper Peninsula told her story. When she stopped, he looked at Alva and asked, "So Alva what's your story and how did a girl from Madrid get to Ann Arbor?"

Alva smiled; she actually giggled a little. "Well, my mom is American." With those words so softly spoken Archie Andersson was bitten by the Love Bug. He listened to her voice and that slight Spanish accent touched with a little Brooklyn brough. And the smile, the smile… It melted the hard scruffy Marine from Petosky, Michigan like the sun melts an icicle, drip by drip. He was in love and struck by her. Not just her beauty, but her grace.

Seth handed the eight-pound eleven-ounce baby boy back to Betsy. Before he did, he whispered to the boy, "I am going to call you Jake son." He had a friend from the Marine Corps whose name was John, but the guys in the band of brothers that are Marines called the poet of a soldier Jake. John Ernest Longfield's nickname would be Jake, or Jakkey till he was older.

Pride, faith, purpose is what Seth felt. He leaned over and kissed the boy as Betsy suckled him his first meal of mother's milk. Someday little Jake would own Archie's Pub and serve mothers milk in a pint glass to the patrons. Guinness was the mother's milk for this Marine.

Warming the Seat

The text to Big Jake read; "New baby arrived. John Ernest Longfield arrived this morning at around 0755." "OMG, being a dad is so cool. ☺ Looking forward to hearing how Carol does in the next week with your first. Did you find out boy /girl ??? Betsy wants to go shopping. LOLOLOL> Give Carol our love. Peace, Love, Sunshine. Bull"

"Thnks, the nation mid-wives tell me it could be Friday or Sautrddy." "1 thng, you will be getting a package tomorrow or the next day. You must accept personally." Jake texted back.`

"KK"

Seth started his routine of wiping down the liquor bottles behind the bar, washing the old mahogany bar.

He felt proud and wondered what his Dad, Mom and Pop were doing right now. Probably all hanging around Betsy and Jakkey. It was almost 10:00am when Archie's opened for beer deliveries.

Seth was excited that tomorrow morning he would pick up his wife and son from the hospital. The new bedroom was ready for the little man.

The next morning, he was up at 0535, he showered and headed out the door to pick up his bride and young son. The discharge did not take long. By 0935 all the Longfield's were home in Indian River. Seth had taken the next four days to be there for Betsy, for Jake, he was in no rush to get back behind the bar.

It was a lazy day for Betsy and her newborn. Feed him, sleep, cuddle her son, feed him and sleep. Seth changed the diapers. Man, he thought baby poop is stinky, laughing. The routine for Betsy and baby repeated itself for the entire day.

By 1530 the ex-Marine was physically drained. He fell asleep in his recliner chair. Seth slept about two hours and did the new dad thing. Change the diapers, rock his boy to sleep so Betsy could recoup and tell the boy stories. Tales of hunting and fishing and reading Nick

Adams. He had spent many a night in combat in the two-hour nap, awake, patrol, rest and patrol. His body kicked into the soldier sleep mode.

Around 1930 he awoke to the smell of bacon. Betsy was slow cooking his favorite brand which would accompany the four scrambled eggs and toast Seth devoured. He was sipping his coffee and finishing his orange juice when the doorbell rang. A little late he thought for FedEx and UPS here in Northern Michigan.

In his cargo shorts, USMC tee and dock siders Seth lumbered to the door. He was surprised. The young man had a wooden lacrosse stick in his right hand and a letter thing rolled like a scroll with a leather strap wound tight around it.

The young man must have been twenty or twenty-one years old. He was dressed in traditional Onondaga clothing. "Mr. Longfield, you might not remember me but I was the boy who played catch with my brother when you and Big Jake returned from war." It has been almost five years since that stay in Onondaga.

The stick was a gift for his son from Chief Elm and Mrs. Owltree. Every boy born on the nation is given his own stick at birth. Seth knew the story as Jake had told him it many times. How lacrosse was the Medicine Game for the Creator. "This sir is an invitation from Chief Elm to join him in the Onondaga Longhouse next Thursday."

Seth untwirled the leather strap and read the message. In Onondaga and across the Six Nations the leaders still used runners to carry the words of the chiefs for important meetings and events. The message was an invitation to attend the Condolence of John Owltree to become a chief of the Onondaga Nation and to sit in the seat his Uncle Orlin had occupied for some fifty-two years. Old Ollie had gone to the spirit world four mouth earlier. Jake had not told Seth he was going to be the new chief of the Wolf Clan and the new Peace Chief who is seated at the right hand of the Tadodaho. The War Chief in charge sat to the Tadodaho's left.

He invited the young lad into his home and offered him food, refreshment and lodging until his return. The young runner accepted the hospitality and then said, "I must return to Onondaga today the chiefs want to know if you will be attending."

Seth said of course yes.

He walked over to his desk just around the corner

from the front door. He took a pencil and wrote on a yellow pad.

"Dear Chief Elm, I and my wife and newborn son will be in Onondaga on Monday evening." Seth was surprised and proud. Big Jake had often been the leader during the many patrols the two had done with other Marines. All the band of brothers looked up to Jake, and Seth.

The Onondaga Runner thanked Seth and excused himself. Ollie Owltree had seven hundred and sixty-seven miles ahead of him according to the F-150's GPS. Seth wished him safe travels and good weather.

The Milk Mom

They had passed Buffalo when the phone rang in the RV Seth had rented. Rather he borrowed it. His golf buddy Jimmy Schall owned an RV Super Store in between Petosky and Mackinaw. The thirty-eight-foot motorhome was like a hotel suite on wheels. Betsy and Jakkey had spent most of the trip resting in the master bedroom. Without the slider engaged it was a small tight safe place for the two to rest, sleep and feed the growing boy.

Seth answered the phone. "Hey brother where are you guys? Mom has dinner started and wants to know." Seth spoke, "We just passed Buffalo and the GPS says two hours and forty-one minutes, give or take." Perfect Jake told him.

"She can't wait to see her new grandbaby dude."

Betsy knew of the ceremony, the title of Bull, the deep loving friendship these two former warriors shared. She was intrigued, she had only been to Onondaga once.

Seth said, "Copy that, tell mom I will see her soon."

His own mother had passed away to breast cancer when he was just sixteen. Aubrey was truly his new mother, the connection to her was the same as he had with his mom Mildred. The road trip was nearing its end. They had stopped for two hours along the way for Betsy and Jakey to chill without the rumble of the road. He had slept too.

A dream had kept running through his brain at least once a week. Seth was riding a huge Centaur like creature with a Buffalo Head. Weird and wild he chuckled.

The sign on the 90 said Syracuse sixteen miles. Seth had the feeling of coming home. The last time he was here was for Carol and Jake's wedding. That was a party like he had never seen.

As they turned the right bend on to I-81 the GPS said four miles. At 1545 they turned off the exit for the ONONDAGA NATION. He told Betsy they were no longer in the United States of America. They were in Onondaga now. The People of the Hills.

Betsy asked to stop at the little grocery store before they went to the Owltree's. She needed more wipes, more diapers and a hairbrush. She had forgotten hers.

After the short pit-stop they drove down Route 11A toward the Onondaga Village. It felt different. She too felt as if they were home, not unlike a new family coming home to visit family and friends. Seth had texted Jake that they had arrived.

As they drove toward the village families came out to the end of their driveways waving and welcoming the Longfield's. Betsy had never witnessed such a welcoming. As they drove deeper into the quaint native community more people were stepping out and waving. Seth slowed the RV to 15 MPH. It was another parade like moment. He thought of the boys tossing the lacrosse ball. The Longhouse and the honor bestowed to him. He thought of Aubrey and her hugs.

Seth turned up Hemlock Road as the RV slid by the Longhouse. The Owltree's lived up near the end of the road in a big cabin Jake's mom and dad had built by hand, log by log cut from the property his mother had title to. Men had no ownership of the Onondaga land. The woman had the land, they were the creators of all humanity. No one really owned the land according to Onondaga Law. The Creator had title to the land, the people were supposed to care for it, honor its gifts and bounty. That was still the practice here on the sovereign Onondaga soil, but not so across the border in the United States.

The RV pulled into the big yard. Jake had pulled four large 2" x 16" x 48" boards from the sawmill he had built. He waved Seth to pull in and ease the big motorhome forward on the boards, and he did. Like in the Marine's Jake was directing.

Jake's brother Edward pulled the long sixty-amp power cord to the big RV and plugged in the shore power, so the Longfield's had electricity. Seth pushed the air brakes on and shut down the coach. He opened the door.

Big Jake said, "Come, come, get Betsy and Jakkey and come with me now brother." Laughing. They followed him into the family clan cabin. There was excitement and a little concern. Jake hugged Betsy and held Jakkey and then Carol walked into the room assisted by Aubrey with a little baby girl born two days prior wrapped in a soft white cotton blanket.

She handed the baby to Jake who was now holding the next generation of these two families. He smiled and kissed his daughter and then kissed Jakkey. He spoke, "John Ernest Longfield meet your first friend Antionette Jackson Owltree." The baby boy and baby girl had bonded, and their hands touched. Jakkey held Antionette's hand, it was bigger than hers and she cooed like a morning dove. He handed the newborns to Aubrey, and she kissed them both holding them close to her chest. And she spoke, "Little Bull meet Morning Dove."

The women quickly deserted Jake and Seth to be alone. Time for the new moms to mother the two new born babes.

The boys sat by the fire which was always burning in this cabin. Jake grasped his brother Seth's hand and spoke. "The fire in this hearth has been burning for over fifty-five years. Never gone out. Like that fire my friend I am asking that the brotherhood we share be like that fire. Always burning, always bring warmth and comfort to those before it."

They told new stories and old ones. He told Seth how it would go down tomorrow in the Longhouse. How all the fifty families of the Haudenosaunee would be in the long house. How the process of being condoled was by clan and then by the nation and then by the confederacy of the Six Nations. Jake walked over to the closet and said "here's my new uniform and cap."

It was a brilliant array of colors and hand sown images. He pulled out the chiefs headdress he would be presented tomorrow. His brother and he had spent all winter assembling the feathers and deer horns, there were two wild turkey feet included.

"What are you wearing tomorrow Marine." Jake asked.

"I brought my dress dude. Only the best for you."

"Does it still fit?" Jake chuckled.

"Like a glove."

Aubrey called out it was dinner time, and the feast began. Venison, wild turkey, fresh caught brook trout, corn chowder, fresh steamed greens from the forest and sweet tea. A green type of tea sweetened with maple water.

Aubrey asked Seth to say the Thanksgiving address. He was befuddled and felt a sense of pride in the request. He stood. The man could talk, he was a publican talking was part of the gig.

When he finished Aubrey passed the first plates to the

new mothers, then the children then Seth and Jake and she was the last to fill her plate.

Betsy was pretty hungry, and she finished first. Jakkey let her know he was hungry. She held him to her chest, raised her shirt and the boy latched onto her right nipple. Dinner time for him.

Annie, as Jake called his new daughter had been fed by Carol, but she was still having trouble getting milk to come. It would come, this was not an uncommon thing. It might take a few hours until she gave milk like a cow does.

Betsy looked at Carol and said, "give me Annie please." She held the little girl only days old to her chest and moved her left nipple into the child's mouth. That was different she thought. Aubrey did not show it, but she noted the special moment. Seth's wife was feeding both children at the same moment. It was a beautiful thing to witness. Once again, Jakkey grabbed Anne's hand.

The Firekeepers

The family dinner was beyond delicious, it was filled with laughter, lore and love.

The women were all clamoring around the two newborn babies and the new Moms. Seth and Jake were to stay tonight in the RV, the women were to enjoy the warmth of the cabin. They had planned to sit by the fire and share the new feeling of being a dad. To speak of the dreams each had wished for as their children entered the world. Jake had built a fire in the big outdoor fire pit. It would be just the two warriors around the glowing flames and embers.

There was a chill in the April spring air. The fire not only warmed their big frames, but it also warmed their spirits too. Both Jake and Seth were not drinkers.

They did enjoy a pint of Guinness when together, but that was Mothers Milk for a Marine. A sandwich in every pint Seth used to joke when they shared the dark milky brew. Seth had bought a four pack of Guinness at the little grocery store. Just a four pack was all they needed.

Both men listened to the other intently as Seth told his fellow Marine all that had happened recently. The passing of his grandfather Archie, the old bottle of French Brandy and that the old man was laid to rest at the end of the runway at Pellston Airport in a little cemetery. How he felt alone sometimes when he cleaned and opened the pub. How he would be taking Jakkey to all the fishing holes to catch trout. To respect the natural world and the gifts it provides. How he and Betsy wanted more children, Seth wanted a girl now.

Jake leaned back on the half log cut bench he had built. He spoke of his Uncle Orlin, whose seat on the council he would occupy like his uncle, for life. Like Seth he too told how Annie would someday be the clan mother. That's what Aubrey had told him when she was born. How the clan mother often knows when the child is born that it will be a leader. Jake looked at Seth and said, "You know John Ernest Longfield is a chief, a leader already?" He felt it so.

Seth had finished his second can of Guinness. Jake had a little left as they sat in the quiet of the night. Jake took the last sip and an owl hooted. It scared the big hulk of Seth's spirit. He almost jumped into the fire. Jake laughed and laughed and laughed. They had a small milk buzz going as Jake used to joke. He took the long iron fire poker and moved the logs around the pit so that they would burn down slowly. It was time for bed.

Both men slept like babies. Seth had the master suite; Jake had the pull-out sofa bed. When they awoke Jake grabbed a towel and tossed it to Seth. Time for our shower pal, he opened the RV door and jumped out in the cold April morning air buck naked. Seth followed him to the outside shower they had rinsed the scars of war upon their return to Onondaga several years earlier.

No breakfast for them today. It was a day of celebration and there would be plenty of food after Jake was made chief. After the boys three S's each dressed in their uniforms for today condolence ceremony. Big Jake in a colorful array of beads sown in his dress shirt, his soon to be headdress was in an old leather covered wood box that would be carried into the Longhouse. Seth looked regal in his Marine Dress Uniform. He put on the Marine Corps white cap and looked in the full-length mirror of the RV. Then he took it off and Jake handed him the leather headband with the two feathers sown in the weave of the leather. Seth let Jake tie it around his head. He had not worn it since he was last in Onondaga. When he was home, he kept it in a special place.

"Where do you keep this when you are in Indian River?" he asked Seth. Seth grinned and told him.

"Well, my grandfather had this ceramic bust of John Wayne in a big cowboy hat. When he died, I took it and it's on the mantle above the fireplace. I tie it on his hat," he said laughing. "I figure that there is a little humor and irony in it." Jake smiled.

The family had gathered outside the cabin. Everyone of the Owltree Clan was in attendance from the elders to the babies. All dressed in traditional clothing. Carol handed Annie to Jake to carry to the longhouse. Betsy held Jakkey, he was dressed up as a young Onondaga boy might be dressed and wrapped in a warm hand sewn blanket with little birds and animals stitched in the cloth. She handed the boy to Seth.

The procession began, the same two boys were having a catch with the lacrosse sticks and ball leading the family down Hemlock Road, young men now. There was singing and laughter as they approached the huge throng of citizens from Onondaga and the other Six Nations. As the duo approached the Onondaga Longhouse there was Chief Elm smiling wide. He and the other Onondaga Chiefs were to welcome Jake and Seth, their newborns in the warriors' arms to the wood stained longhouse.

Jake and Seth knew the routine. Stand at attention as the Tadodaho spoke and delivered the Thanksgiving Address. He welcomes the two new children to the nation. Chief Elm motioned for Jake to step forward. He did so and handed Annie to the chief who raised the young newborn and gave praise to the Creator. Then he motioned Seth over and he repeated the praise of the Creator. Then the mothers of the two babies and the Onondaga women moved off to begin the preparations for the dinner and celebrations later in the day.

The chief welcomed Seth and Jake into the longhouse. Seth noticed that the benches were tight to the walls so all the chiefs of the fifty families of the Haudenosaunee had a place to sit. In the middle of the longhouse was one lone wood chair. Chief Elm motioned Jake to sit there. Seth stood to Jake's right not knowing where to sit or stand.

Chief Elm slowly walked up to his place on the east end of the longhouse centered between the other chiefs. This was the Grand Council of the Iroquois Confederacy. Each of the Six Nations had representation on the Grand Council. They were the "Firekeepers", the central body of Haudenosaunee government and laws. They were all seated except Chief Elm, he stood and spoke.

"We gather here today to welcome a new member to our council fire, to listen, to think, to honor those who came before him. He is a great warrior who has fought for freedom, for our nation and theirs. Today he will leave his weapons under the great pine tree as our ancestors did when we formed this confederacy, this union. Today he becomes our peace chief. For a man who has been to war and knows the ravages and the sorrow of war also knows the way to peace." All the chiefs nodded in agreement. There was no red or blue in the congregation of leadership like in America. The Six Nations were united on many things, not everything. Democracy in Indian Land and the United States was not easy it had to be nurtured and must given space to grow.

The Tadodaho motioned for Seth to step forward. The space to the right of Chief Elm was empty. This is where Chief Orlin Owltree had sat.

Elm spoke, "Bull, you are a special human son. And in our nation, our confederacy, we don't often invite ancestors of the colonists who stole our lands into the longhouse. However today, today we do something that has only been done once before in the longhouse. Today son, you will warm the seat of Chief Owltree until he is condoled." The leader put his two hands on Seth's shoulders and turned him to face the assembly of leadership. The chief to his left stood and handed Chief Elm a lone Eagle Feather. The chief threaded the quill end into Bull's headdress.

"Bull from now on you will be Chief Bull Longfield. You too are a peace chief and a man we trust with our heritage and existence on Great Turtle Island."

Seth was struck with honor, fear, a feeling of deep responsibility. Chief Elm motioned him to sit in the future place his brother Jake would occupy and warm the seat. The chiefs of the Fifty Families of the Haudenosaunee stood and applauded the new appointment. It was a historic emotional moment.

Smoke of the Fire

The Condolence Ceremony was wrapping up. The chiefs had welcomed Jake to the Council. They had celebrated his journey.

There was business to be done too. Each Nation representative spoke of their nation's ideas, positions on important items, on keeping the colonists advances from further taking the freedoms granted to them by the Creator. Of their lands which were taken illegally but were still legally Iroquois Land under the Treaty of Fort Stanwick.

Seth had been given a thick leather binder which held a document that confirmed it was their land. Inside was a copy of the *Everett Report* which was written in 1922. It summarized the history of the Haudenosaunee loss of those lands. The document was commissioned by the

New York State Attorney General and the Secretary of New York State to determine the status of the American Indian in New York State.

Assemblyman Everett had been charged with leading a delegation to all Six Nations to listen to the history from the Indian perspective. To record the view from the Native American side. New York State had fiscal obligations to the Haudenosaunee as each year payments were made; muslin and salt were exchanged as per the Treaty. New York wanted to know what the cost going forward might be to its taxpayers.

The Grand Council wanted to know what Seth's views were once he read the entire document. He was to take his time. No need to rush he was told; we were here long before they came; and we will be here long after they are gone.

The celebration had begun outside the longhouse. All the chiefs stepped though the doorway and awaited the two new chiefs to leave the council of the longhouse fire and be welcomed by the people.

It was a grand time of dance, people laughing and singing the old songs, good food and cheer.

Sometime around 9:15 the two new chiefs, the two new moms and their next generation headed up Hemlock Road. to the cabin. It was time for bed.

Let the Truth Be Told

Seth had tucked his wife and child into bed. Jakkey was in a wood handmade crib Big Jake had crafted six months earlier when he knew he would become chief. Jake and Carol were cuddled in their room at the cabin, Annie in the exact same style crib as Jakkey.

Aubrey was by the fire sitting and reading a book. "*To Become a Human Being*" was written by the Tadodaho prior to Chief Elm. Leon Shenandoah was a great leader, a small framed man with an empathy and knowledge like no other. He had noted the things which the old chief thought important to be a good human.

Seth had read the book; he was given a copy back on the day he left Onondaga after his discharge from the Marine Corps. He remembered he thought every human being should get a copy of this book when they are born. Like an Onondaga boy being given a lacrosse stick at birth.

He sat next to Aubrey, she smiled.

"So, Bull, kind of a wonderful and wild day…"

"Yes Mom, I, I didn't expect that today."

"Well, we Clan Mothers think you earned the title son. So did Jake." She handed Seth the copy, her copy of the ninety-four pages of wisdom. "This is Little Bulls; you can read it to him at night as he falls asleep and dreams." Seth was taken by her love and trust in him.

He rose and kissed her on the forehead. Chief Bull had some reading to do. Seth excused himself to the RV.

The coach was warm and peaceful, it had a been a wonderful experience today. But he needed alone time to take in what had transpired today, what had been asked of him to do, to be.

He settled into the nice leather recliner in the coach and opened the leather binder. Inside was a document that was three and a half inches thick of a photocopied summary of the status of the Indian.

He flipped the first page and started reading.

It was nearly daylight when he flipped the last page.

The sun was rising to the east of the nation above the hills. The morning songbirds were singing as the morning mist rose above the forest.

Seth stepped out to the morning splendor and breathed in the cold crisp air. He did not see the old chief sitting by the fire. He heard him say, "How'd you sleep Bull?"

Seth rubbed his eyes and yawned. "I didn't. I read the report, just finished it."

"I knew you would read it last night. That's why I stayed up too. I wanted to sit by the fire here and listen to what you think." Seth sat and pondered what the hell to say. Then he spoke.

"Pretty much says it's your land west of Fort Stanwix. I mean when the Attorney General and the Secretary of State for New York apologize and says its Indian Land and then tell you that it is not they are blowing smoke up someone ass."

Elm laughed and chuckled. "So, what you think we should do?"

"I am not sure Chief. Jake and I have a friend who was a marine lawyer. He was a few years older than us and mustered out with us. The guy was a constitutional lawyer. They offered him a job with the US Attorney Office, but he declined. Let me see what he thinks." Chief Elm rose and put his hand on Seth's right shoulder.

"That's why I asked you to be a peace chief Seth. To council me on how we might regain oversight of our lands. No one owns the land; the Creator gives us permission to only take what we need to survive and thrive. We don't want anyone's land, but we do want to have some level of input on how our lands are used. How we make sure that in Seven Generations our children's children, your children's, children's, children can live in peace and in a world that is safe for all."

They both smelled the bacon cooking in the cabin. Seth stood and the two chiefs walked together toward the warm joyful sounds from within the cabin. Time for breakfast.

Article II

The week at Onondaga had filled his spirit and soul with love and family. The bonding of the Longfield's and the Owltree's would cross the boundaries of Onondaga and beyond. Over the sixteen-hour drive home Seth had run the facts through his head over and over. It was their land, and they had no standing. They, the Onondaga Nation had never been part of the United States of America.

Of all the Native People's Reservations across USA the only truly sovereign soil recognized by the government of the United States was Onondaga. No federal official could enter the nation and arrest an Onondaga Citizen. If there was a need for police, they had to work through the protocols no different than that of wanting to arrest someone wanted in the US, who was in Canada.

What would have Archie thought? If he had read the Everett Report, would he understand and see the obvious…

The Longfield's had settled back into the log home Seth had designed and his friend's construction company built. Betsy and Jakkey were napping as Seth sat by his fireplace holding the leather brief. He grabbed his cell phone and called Niles. That's who Archie would call if he had the same questions as Seth.

Seth laughed as he thought of Niles phone ringing the first four bars of God Bless America. One day when Niles and Archie were sitting at the bar, Seth had used Betsy's phone to keep calling Niles's phone so the music would play. It was a hilarious few moments. Niles answered, "Ayup, this in Niles how may I help you?"

"When did you get back? I was wondering how the week went. The baby and Bets travel well?" Seth told him a brief summary of the week and that he needed to speak with Niles. If he wasn't busy, would he stop by the pub tomorrow early as Seth was cleaning and prepping opening the doors. "Bring that old copy of the constitution with you." Seth hung up the phone.

Niles had told Arch that he would keep an eye on Seth till he joined him in Heaven someday.

"See you tomorrow kiddo."

Seth felt at ease, as if a ten-pound bag had been lifted from his shoulders.

The next day Seth was wiping down the bottles of spirits and the mahogany bar when he heard Niles come through the back door. It was a little past 0830. Seth poured two cups of coffee and pulled a bottle of Irish Wiskey from behind the bar. He poured a little in both cups of the morning warmth.

The barkeep slid the coffee over to Niles as Niles slid over a small, tattered book. Seth turned it around and read the cover. The United States Constitution, Seth was sworn to uphold. Niles took a little sip of the coffee touched with a bit of Irish Wisdom.

"Article II Section 2, take a moment to read it."

Seth opened the small yet powerful words of the people. This was the law of the land. The basis for all laws that followed. He read the section of the Constitution. *"He shall have the power, by and with the Advice and Consent of the Senate, to make Treaties, provided two thirds of the Senators present concur..."*

Niles spoke. "So, the president negotiates treaties with other nations and the Senate by majority of two-thirds ratifies the treaty. The first treaty of the United States of America after the Revolution of 1776 was with the Iroquois Nations. All treaties enacted since then stand on the cornerstone of that treaty."

Seth let the information sink in for a minute and asked a question. "So, when did that treaty expire?" Niles chuckled, "It didn't, still exists although it's neglected by the courts." He went on to relay that this original Treaty with the Iroquois had been amended and negotiated with one of the final Treaties being the Treaty of Fort Stanwix signed in 1784 by the representatives of the Six Nations and the fledgling new democracy of the Colonists. The Treaty was ratified by the Senate and became that cornerstone.

Niles spoke further. "You asked me why they seemed to lose every time the Onondaga's went to state or federal courts seeking relief. The answer is simple. They have no standing here. None. They are Switzerland, Japan, Britain; they are an independent and sovereign nation. Separate from the good ole USA." He went on the discuss further that the Swiss can't sue in state or federal courts, Japan can't, "hell Canada can't, and they are right next door."

Seth pondered a moment. Niles could see his brain grinding on the information he had just learned from a judge. The old man noticed the glow when the light bulb went off in Seth's mind. "I have standing, you have standing right?"

Niles sat up on his bar stool and smiled. "Yes, any American Citizen can bring forth a complaint or action against anyone, any level of government from state to the feds."

Niles smiled, the publican in Seth smiled a devious humorous smile. "Niles, I want to sue the state of New York, the federal executive branch, the congress and the US courts to require recognition and enforcement of the treaties or treaty of 1784."

They sat there in the quiet of the pub Archie had built, loved and cherished. Archie also was a purest with right and wrong, good and bad, and above all doing the right thing even if it is causing you discomfort. Seth remembered those teachings; they were part of genetics. He would sue and stand before the courts.

"You got any old friends who are good lawyers judge?

Sounds like I might need one or two." Both laughed. Niles could feel his old friend Arch's spirit in the boy.

"Ayup, I do. And you aren't the plaintiff, Seth. Not being a new peace chief in the Onondaga Nation, even if it was a ceremonial appointment. I am filing the lawsuits. And if your grandfather was sitting here next to me, he would probably sign on too."

Niles Gunderson would call his favorite former judge. Jimmy Fitzgibbons, "Fitzi" as Niles and the other jurists called the plump Irish legend. Fitzi was now retired from the bench and practicing law for a firm in Chicago. He actually summered on Lake Michigan in a cottage, well it was bigger than a cottage overlooking the lake by Traverse City.

James Morris Fitzgibbons was a true Irish Ball Busting man who loved his children and grandchildren first and foremost and then second on the list was the law. Fitzi loved the law. He and Niles had spent many a night sipping whiskey and eating venison summer sausage with a piece of extra sharp Northern Michigan Cheddar Cheese talking about the laws and constitution. He was a constitutional nerd Niles chuckled as he told that to Seth.

Niles pulled his flip phone from the old wool coat that

had been stitched on in places. If he was standing on the corner in Chicago folks might have tossed a buck or two in his cap thinking he was a homeless man.

The phone rang twice and then Niles heard that gruffed deep voice of his buddy Fitzi. They exchanged the normal pleasantries. Fitzi telling Niles he was still full of shit and Niles telling the plump barrister he was the king of crap too. Seth stood there knowing that something good was about to happen.

Niles asked if he and Seth could get some time, legal time. "I don't want any of your charity pro bono bullshit Fitzi, we'll pay you what your time is worth. Let's get it straight right now. I don't want a bill mailed to me unexpectedly. I will pay you $9.87 per hour. That's the minimum wage here in Michigan." Almost laughing his way to another angina attack the lawyer agreed. With one caveat.

"No checks you old son of a gun. Just cash only from you."

Wetting a Line

The current of the little brook above Walloon Lake was running swift with the rains of early May. Trout fishing here in Northern Michigan was an artful pursuit. Like Ernest Hemingway Niles, Archie and now Seth had fished for that elusive fish.

Seth was orchestrating a brilliance with a fly rod that the old judge had never witnessed. Swinging the fly rig back and forth with the bucktail fly dancing on the wind until he had the perfect cast to hit the water where the biggest fish would be. The fly drifted down the stream as Niles meandered over and sat on the log next to Fitzi. "That boy can throw a fly Niles."

The lawyer was enjoying charging Niles $9.87 an hour

to fish. He didn't care if he caught a damn fish or cold. He spoke to Niles...

"So, I read the report thing. I looked over Article II, Section 2 of the Constitution. And in my humble opinion it is pretty much an open and shut case. They own the land west of Fort Stanwix." He handed Niles his flask of craft distilled whiskey. Niles took a swill. "MMM, MMM that's really good!"

Fitzi detailed that his daughter's brother-in-law had a little distillery near Oak Park that made this special barrel spirit. "It's called The Judgement."

The old men discussed the aspects of the case. The law was pretty damn clear. But getting the court to be true to the law and genuine to the treaty was the dilemma. Niles reached into his pocket and pulled out nine hundred and eighty-eight dollars and handed it to Fitzi. He knew his purpose, knew his time left here on the planet was to do the right thing. And he would.

"Here is the first hundred hours of compensation. I want a detailed invoice showing you did the work." Fitzi handed him back the flask and they both took a big swill.

Seth hooked a big fish and was working it hard. He

walked the beast from the depths of the creek to the shallows. Slowly gaining ground on the fish until it was flopping on the sandy bank of the Bear River in the hamlet of Walloon Lake.

Niles looked at Fitzi and said, "I want a receipt too."

They would share the big brooky tonight at Niles cabin. Niles had an idea of where to file the lawsuit too.

The fire crackled as the three men sat around the hearth. Seth drinking a ginger-ale on ice and the two old judges sipping some of Niles Irish Whiskey. Seth listened; he had much to learn. Fitzi was detailing the process of filing the four notices of claim in the New York Courts and the US First District Court of Northern New York in Albany. The timeline would be slow once filed the former judge detailed. Justice moves slowly like an iceberg heading south.

Then he spoke to Seth. "So, you're the one whose idea it was to sue everybody?" Fitzi and Niles chuckled a little good buzz laugh. "Yes sir" Seth said sheepishly.

It was a good plan Fitzi told Seth. One that will make them think how they defend and deflect this multi-angle assault on democracy. "We'll use their own words and actions against them to the point that when they open their mouths, they be supporting Niles's claim." Seth asked how long...

"I figure we go through the first level of the federal courts in New York's Northern District, and it eventually ends up at the Supreme Court one day. Probably four to six years till that happens." Niles chuckled. "I guess I better started eating healthier if I am going to make it to ninety-four or five."

It was almost 2230 when the two old friends retired for the evening. Seth sat by the fire. He texted Jake.

"J thnk I have the answer."

"Call me"

He opened the old, tattered copy of the Constitution. The words he had sworn to uphold and defend with his life must be true and genuine, his minds voice whispered. Men and women died for these simple defining prose of democracy.

His phone chirped; it was Jake calling him.

"He brother, I am here in Niles cabin. He and his old judge lawyer friend just went to sleep after a day of fishing Bear River and dining on a big brooky I caught. How's Mom, Carol and Annie doing?"

Jake told him all was well in Onondaga. The weather

was bringing in the warmth and the spring rains were leading to the blooms of May. He had settled in as the new chief of his clan and the Onondaga Nation.

"How about you? Been up to anything fun or monumental up there in Northern Michigan?"

Seth smiled and chuckled. "You ever read the US Constitution Jake?" Sure, he replied. "Well, I have been reading it a lot lately. Niles gave me his copy a few weeks back. He was a town judge in Walloon for like two decades. He pointed out Article II, Section 2. You familiar with it?" Jake wondered about the karma of the moment.

"Yes, Chief Elm and I were discussing it today. We have grievances."

Seth told him about his discovery. And of Niles desire to file lawsuits to bring recognition and enforcement of the Treaties.

"I need you and Chief Elm to fly to Pellston Airport tomorrow and I will pick you up. I want to go over the actions we are taking. Don't tell him anything other than I found the answer to the question he asked me at the firepit, OK?"

The Hills of Walloon

A little red cardinal flew over and landed on the tombstone of Archibald and Alva Andersson. Seth was struck by the natural emotion of the red bird landing on the old pilots headstone as the plane from Detroit lowered its landing gear heading towards the runway. Seth checked his watch, 1243 maritime. Right on time.

He had stopped to chat with Archie about what Niles had planned in the coming days. Asking his great grandfather for his blessing on holding his nation to account, to ensure a better world for his, Jake's and Arch's generations yet to be born. He looked up at the next plane landing imagining in his mind that the aircraft was piloted by Archie.

Seth headed to the gate pick up area in front of the

small quaint air terminal. There was no traffic cop waving you on. He parked outside the terminal and stepped from the pick-up standing as a Marine at ease. Seth wore his denim blue jeans. Wrangler was his brand, a navy-blue deep plaid flannel shirt, Keene hiking boots.

He was beaming in the early day sunlight. His hair was still that buzz sided Marine cut with a small thick bristle style top cut. The image of Jarhead would be appropriate if someone had the balls to call him on his choice of hair style.

He spotted Chief Elm first, Jake was trailing behind the world leader hauling two wheeled travel suitcases with his backpack strapped to his back. It was the old military issue backpack from his last tour of duty. It was worn and carried the memories of war times. Seth hugged Chief Elm and welcomed him to Northern Michigan, the territory of the Odawa Indian Nation.

Jake strolled up next and gave Seth a big bear hug.

Jake loaded up the luggage as Seth held the front passenger door open for the Tadodaho as Jake jumped in the back seat of the dually pickup truck.

"We're headed to Niles's cabin on Walloon Lake chief. He'll have some lunch and a fire in the hearth going."

"Did you call the chief of the Odawa Seth? I need to let him know I am in his lands. It would be a great level of dis-respect if I did not call on him or inform him of my visit." Seth told him that Niles had called the chief, he and the chief had fought many a fire together as volunteers here in the most northern tip of Michigan near Petosky. Dinner had been set for the evening where the two leaders would share the creator's bounties.

The old chief smiled; he had picked the right man to be his second chief of peace. Elm's grin did not reveal his inner satisfaction. Seth was learning to be the chief that Chief Elm needed without teaching or guidance. He was acting on his own personal values. Aubrey had been right; she always was but he could not let her know that. It was a game the two siblings played on each other.

As they pulled down Lake Grove Road, Seth pulled up to a small white cottage just over the knoll in the road. "That's the Hemingway Cottage where Grace and Clarence Hemingway summered at and raised Ernest, his brother Leicester and the Hemingway sisters." Jake stepped out and stood on the road absorbing the environment, the air, the warmth of the sun as it shown down through the towering trees. Seth popped his head out the driver's side window. "Niles' cabin is just up the road. Hop in and we'll get you two settled."

Jake wanted some space. "I will walk the rest of the way Seth. I will find Niles place." Seth put the truck in drive and slowly pulled around the next curve losing Jake in the rearview mirror. Jake also wanted Seth to have a few moments with Chief Elm to inform him of his answer to the "question."

They pulled down the small, crushed stone lane to the cabin and pulled into the spot Seth always parked. He shut off the truck and turned to Elm.

"I have the answer chief. You may not like the facts, but they are what they are. And if you agree we can change the outcome I believe."

"Well Bull the truth is the truth. It's the lies that hurt people, the truth can only bruise you."

Seth asked a stupid question. "So, you have read our Constitution, I am sure more than once." Elm smiled as Seth continued. "Well Article II, Section 2; of the constitution states, "He shall." Elm stopped him.

"You mean this little gem of a book Bull." He hands Seth his old, tattered copy of the US Constitution. Seth was shocked, actually dumbfounded. "You didn't think

I knew your laws, huh? This what you talking about?" Elm held the book open to Article II, Section 2 and slid it over to Seth.

"Yes, sir. That's it."

"What about it Bull?"

Seth detailed in depth his theory. They were a sovereign nation like Switzerland, Germany, Japan, China and every other people with a formal government. And Onondaga was the only original sovereign nation with sovereign lands prior to the Act of Repatriation of Indian lands to Indians in 1987. Then he delivered the dagger to the dilemma of the denials in the courts.

"You have no standing…"

"You can sue all you want; they will entertain your filing and kick it around a few years. Then when you think maybe, just maybe we can gain a little ground. They kick it to the curb."

He could see Elm's mind sizzling with the confrontation of the fact. Seth was right.

And then Seth spoke, "But I have standing, Niles has standing, and he is going to file actions to require the United States Government to recognize the Treaty of Fort Stanwix and to enforce the treaty as well." He told Elm that Niles had offered to file the actions knowing Seth would, but his ceremonial position as a Peace Chief of the Onondaga Nation might provide the government with an excuse to have the cases thrown out on technical issues. They could not throw out an action filed by an American Citizen who was a decorated former Coastie, former town judge and volunteer fireman. It would not hurt that he was also a retired physical education instructor and history teacher at the Petosky Public School District. Niles had taught for forth-three years.

Niles had told Seth that at some point he would be needed to negotiate as the peace chief for the American's and the Onondaga's.

Chief Elm looked at Seth and spoke once more. "Well. That requires a little re-evaluation of the facts then. What does Niles propose?"

Seth said let's have lunch and then we can sit with Niles and his lawyer. The lawyer has some questions for you and Jake.

Chew The Fat

The was charcoal grill full of hot fresh coals. Niles loved to grill meat or anything edible really. He had a nice Weber gas grill outside the back door of the kitchen under a little roofed entry and walkway. There was a charcoal grill that was located five steps beyond on a big stone tabletop resting on a concrete pad. Niles made the best damn burgers on the planted. He called them "Gundy Burgers".

The old man loved his cheeseburgers and homemade Russet kettle cooked chips. He had sliced and fried the chips as Seth was heading to the airport. Now it was time for the chef to do his magic with a burger. Seth had told him Chief Elm loved cheeseburgers too, plain with cheddar cheese and a toasted roll. Jake strolled down the lane as the chief and Seth were walking into the cabin.

Seth winked at Jake. "ALL GO."

That was a signal from the past that all things were good, time to kick it gear for the battle of the day. As the old chief entered the cabin he felt at home. It was not really a cabin. It was a big, beautiful log home, five bedrooms, with a grand parlor and field stone hearth. Off to the other side of the great room was the dining room. There was a small study with shelves of books and books and books. It seems Niles is a reader to thought Elm.

Introductions were made and handshakes exchanged. Seth excused himself to get the chiefs travel luggage. The Chief would be staying with Niles and Fitzi for the two scheduled nights of council by the hearth. Jake was staying with the Longfield's in Indian River. Betsy wanted a hug and Jake wanted to play with Jakkey. The men had their burgers and chips.

They then sat by the hearth, Elm was telling the story of the Peacemaker. How the original Five Nations buried their weapons under the pine tree to form the first democracy in the Western Hemisphere around 944 AD. That was the carbon dating of the leather piece found with the Pine Tree inscribed. Science confirmed the date not some old Indian tale.

Elm told them of the 1797 Handsome Lake Prophecy. A message from the Creator on the Seven Generations principles. How if man did not listen to Mother Earth, and recognize we are only here to care for the land and creatures in seven generations things would be changing. Like the trees dying from the top, the fish jumping from the streams because the water was bad and that the fires of the sun would burn down on the earth if we as a people did not heed the call of nature.

Then he spoke of the treaties, the lies and deception of the colonists that was documented in the Everett Report.

When he stopped the chief had spoken for some nearly two hours. He turned to Niles and then to Fitzi and asked, "So if we have no standing how can we help?"

Fitzi smiled, it was that sweet Irish Chicago smile. A wide grin like a brown bear thought Elm. In his gruffy and deep voice the lawyer spoke. He had listened the entire time, deeply. Elm could tell that.

Fitzi cleared his throat.

"Well in reading the treaty, in reviewing the Everett

Report and reading my constitution. In my learned and honest opinion, it…"

He sipped his coffee cup of Irish wisdom.

"It's your land, Open and Shut, Period!"

He explained the challenge is to get the government to admit that and then to allow some level of oversight on the environmental and natural use of resources and the land. He would lay out the case on two simple principles which he detailed.

The old chief shook his head. He understood.

Jimmy Fitzgibbons nodded to Seth. "Tell him your idea." He did. How the objective was to get the government to want to negotiate or parley on the old existing treaty. They had to acknowledge it, it still was real, still valid as a legal and lawful treaty. But would they give up some inclusion of the native people in the oversight of the land. That was the question to be answered.

Seth smiled and spoke definitively.

"I will make them an offer they cannot refuse. To steal a line from The Godfather." The six men chuckled and laughed.

Chief Elm looked at Niles and spoke. "It's your battle for our rights and lands. What can we do to help?"

Fitzi said softly, "nothing. If needed I may call you or a member of the Onondaga Nation to testify to the truth as you know it. Nothing more, nothing less. I am the one who will hand them a load of bullshit and make then wish that the stink of the past treatment of your people was washed from their souls."

Elm filled his corncob pipe and lit it. The smoke swirled around his head and the gathering of minds.

"Please if we can assist let Bull know. He knows the path to take on this uncharted journey."

"How much is Niles paying you for this work, if I can ask." Niles smiled. "I am paying him minimum wage in Michigan, $9.87 per hour." Elm laughed and said, "is he worth it?" Niles said, "he's worth every dam penny and more."

Penny saved is a penny earned, right. Thought the former Coastie.

A State Dinner

The two Onondaga chiefs had walked down the stone path and sat silently in two chairs on Niles dock. Seth and Niles were prepping for the dinner to be served at the official Indian state style dinner.

Seth had made Aubrey's famous corn chowder and Betsy had pre-cooked seven of her famous baked potato smash for Seth to slide in the oven at three hundred seventy-five degrees for thirty minutes.

The charcoal grill was started. Tonight, Niles would be doing his grill master task of roasting a fresh Buffalo tenderloin Jake had brought with a Venison backstrap from late December off a sweet two-year-old doe Seth had dropped with his muzzleloader. Meat, potatoes, good company and Seth's last epicurean delight, his mixed greens salad with the homemade balsamic vinegar and olive oil with his special seasonings. Betsy had made a maple apple pie for dessert.

Seth stepped on the porch and rang the little triangle. He tapped it lightly and yelled down to the dock. "Our visitors should be here in fifteen…"

The old chief and his new Peace Chief headed to the cabin full of Mother Nature's bounties for their peaceful stay by the lake. Neither had really spoken about anything. They just sat devouring the view, late afternoon sunshine and peace of the shores on Walloon Lake. Seth had let Dusty out and he stopped at his favorite tree. The old dog strolled up to Chief Elm and accompanied the world leader to the cabin like a sentry walking along side.

A few minutes later the Odawa leader, Chief Jacobi Durant, and his Peace Chief were welcomed into the warmth of the cabin. The aroma of the kitchen and the wood fireplace was enchanting. Niles welcome both men and introduced the others who would be joining this unique meeting of two Native Nations. Elm motioned everyone to sit by the fire as he spoke the Thanksgiving Address. It was the short version, only about twelve minutes. He lit a small sprinkling of tobacco in the little bowl Niles had set on the end table. An offering to the Creator, asking for guidance, peace, good health and a good mind for making the right decisions.

Niles told the two guests of his plan to sue his nation. He was going to check the coals for grilling the meat and excused himself. Fitzi spoke next, Niles had handed him the turkey feather, one of many in a little vase above the hearth on the mantle.

Lawyer Fitzgibbons summarized his approach without getting down to the deep details he had told Elm, Jake, Seth and Niles.

Then Elm asked the two Odawa's how the hunting and fishing was here in Northern Michigan. The chief told of the changes in nature due to global warming and that the cycle of life was disturbed. They still filled the store house and freezer with meat from the deer and fish from the lakes. But the growing cycle for the "three sisters", corn, squash and beans; and that the fruit and greens and sweet berries of the land were facing unprecedented rains, along with hot dry periods in the summer. The changes threatened the Odawa citizen way of life and sustenance.

Seth strolled in from the kitchen and asked everyone to be seated in the dining room. The grub was ready.

Niles brought the meats hot off the grill as Seth placed the potatoes and salad bowl on the beautiful Stickley table. Niles sat at his place at the end. Seth at the other Fitzi, Jake and Elm to Niles right and Chief Durant and Chief Devin Lake to his left. He asked everyone to join hands as he had done every night with his family and Debbie giving thanks for all God gives us.

The Wise Men and the Star

The old Coastie knew his stars. In the United States Coast Guard, Niles had been a navigator who would use a sexton to figure out where the ship was out at sea. He knew his constellations. The Coastie, the lawyer and the Indian Chief sat on the dock below Niles lake home. Niles with his Marlboro Reds, Elm with his Corncob Pipe and Fitzi with a nice fresh Cuban Cigar sat there pondering the day and letting the dinner settle.

Niles asked the Chief what constellations were the important ones for he and his people.

Chief Elm showed him the bear and the other eleven spirits in the stars. It was a dark night with just a little sliver of the new moon showing above the horizon. The air was chilling, and the lake was quiet.

Elm asked Niles how the fishing was in the lake? Good year-round Niles replied. How the hunting was in the fall? Niles still hunted; he did not shoot much anymore as Seth was the masterful hunter now. And then he asked him why?

Why would an eighty-eight-year-old man decide to sue his nation on the behalf of another?

Niles lit another Marlboro Red. He let the smoke waft up from the cigarette and smiled. "Well, my wife Debbie, rest her soul, was the one who taught me about being of purpose. Of doing things for others, because you can, and you should. She's still my inspiration. And Seth is my God Son, Debbie was his God Mother and God willing it is still my job and hers to protect him from harm."

He went on to detail how Seth was the one who figured it out. That the treaty was still valid, Article II, Section 2 and that The *Everett Report* thoroughly details that the land is the Haudenosaunee. Then he spoke of his directing Seth to allow him to file the notices of claim. That Seth must listen and learn, and then listen more.

Chief Elm thanked Niles and asked him one more question. "And what will you being the plaintiff allow Seth to do once he is done listening?"

Niles chuckled and passed the conversation over to Fitzi. "Fitzi, you tell him Seth's role." The gruff voice of the old lawyer smiled and said, "Peace Chief, Seth or as you folks call him Chief Bull will be the voice of reason, the voice of peace for your land and ours. When the government is at the last stand, backs against the walls we offer peace."

"Rather we recommend that Seth who is recognized as a warrior in the United States and Onondaga be the leader of the discussion on the peace and recognition of the treaty and laws."

Elm pondered and spoke. "And why would your Supreme Court allow that Fitzi?"

Fitzi looked up at the stars.

"I wish I may I wish I might have the wish I have tonight." He winked at Niles and delivered the secret sauce to that question. "Well, the Chief Justice of the Supreme Court is a Marine, all Marines, all of them are brothers sworn to uphold the Constitution of the United States of America with their lives, bodies and souls."

Chief Elm looked at both wise men and nodded. "I trust Bull with our lives and the lives of the Seven Generations yet to come. But will your courts allow that?"

Fitzi replied, "they will be looking for a way to save face globally on this first ever treaty that George Washington signed."

Niles asked if they would join him in prayer. He did not pray often but when he did it was from his heart and soul. In the quiet of Walloon Lake, a loon called out to its loving partner. COO, CAACOO, COO, COO, COO… Niles knew his Debbie was near.

"Dear God and our Creator. Please give us three old wise men the blessing you gave the three wise men on their journey to greet your son to the world in that little stable. Bless our leaders and all people of our nations with good health and wellness, with wisdom and character. Give strength to those who need it and be mindful of those who would use their strength to harm others. The greatest strength is gentleness, I am told. Please bless my God Son with the gentleness of a hummingbird and the strength of the bull."

Not another word was spoken for the next ten minutes as the three old men finished their smokes. What more was there to say…

Across the Bow

Fitzi had filed the three federal legal actions against the executive, legislative and judicial branches of the United States in Albany, New York. Albany was known as the First District of the Northern New York Federal Courts. The First District was the first of the federal courts in the United States.

In the three years, seven months and fourteen days since the filings the court had directed the judicial proceedings to be moved to Syracuse, New York where there was a slew of federal judges and magistrates. The honorable Nolan Dyer McNally was the senior judge. Judge McNally had been assigned to the proceedings. Nolan McNally was a former Air Cavalry member in Vietnam who then became a federal prosecutor and was appointed by President Bush.

Both Fitzi and the lawyers from the United States had submitted documents, briefs and evidence to the court. Early on in the process Seth had reached out to Wallace "Walli" Gibney, the Marine lawyer he and Jake had befriended while serving together. He was a constitutional nerd of a barrister and Fitzi loved having him at his side.

Today was a big day. Judge McNally was entertaining a motion for dismissal filed by the government. Fitzi and Walli had been waiting for this moment. This chink in the armor, and they were ready for battle.

The court clerk stood. She was a tall woman.

"All rise, the First District Court of Northern New York is now in session. The Honorable Nolan McNally presiding."

Nolan Dyer McNally was a third generation Irishman whose family was based on Syracuse's historic Tipperary Hill. He was a distinguished judge who still enjoyed a pint of Guinness at Kitty Hoynes, his favorite pub on a Friday after a week's work.

McNally brought the court to order and asked the government to address their motion. When they were completed Fitzi was given his time to respond.

"Your honor, the question of the governments filing

for dismissal seems to define their lack of courage to address the issues before this court. Mr. Gunderson's filing is a legitimate request for the court to consider the law, the existing treaty, or treaties and I ask that you sir allow that today to move forward. For the government to argue before the court and allow my clients reasoning for the filings to be address."

Judge McNally removed his glasses and pondered. He was cornered by the plump Irishman from Chicago.

"Motion denied. Gentlemen, we will proceed today. Mr. Fitzgibbons you may begin." Seth had his notebook, he would make a check next to the three words written down. The courts, the government, Fitzi. Checkmark for Fitzi and the court.

Chief Elm, Aubrey and Jake sat on the right side of the court behind Fitzi, Walli and Niles. Seth sat on the left side behind the governments law team of four. He wished he could sit in the aisle, in a neutral position.

Fitzi entered into the record the replica Two Row Wampum, The Wampum for the 1744 Treaty of Lancaster and the governments copy. A replica of the Silver Chain and the thick binder containing the Everett Report. The last was the Treaty of Fort Stanwix from 1784 along with a period map showing the border between the United States and Haudenosaunee lands. There were treaties after Fort Stanwix, those agreements fell upon the cornerstone of the Two Row Wampum and the Stanwix Treaties.

The government lawyers began their arguments for keeping the enforcement at bay. To delay and misdirect the decision for the court. The court had taken depositions from Chief Elm regarding his understanding of the treaties, of their honoring the agreement and of the United States continued lack of acknowledgement of Native Rights.

Fitzi read portions of the Elm Deposition.

Seth had kept his checkmarks going. The tally was Fitzi seven, the court six and the government four checkmarks. Niles' lawyer was working his magical wisdom. Of the six court checkmarks four were in Fitzi' favor.

Fitzi was standing with his yellow pad pealed back making another jab at the government position. He asked that he be allowed to call more witnesses to prove the standing of the Native oversight.

The lead government attorney, Robert Frederickson rose and objected.

"Mr. Fitzgibbons, you can call all the witnesses you like sir. And I will call mine."

Walli motioned to Fitzi to read what he had just written down. Fitzi smiled, a big broad smile.

Judge McNally looked at Niles and then Fitzi and then at Frederickson.

"Mr. Fitzgibbons do you have any witnesses to bring before the court?"

"I do sir, may I approach the bench?"

"Certainly, Mr. Frederickson would you step forward as well please."

The two lawyers and the judge began a discussion that went on for almost two minutes. It seemed like thirty to Seth. And Fitzi slid over the yellow pad. The name Gerard Lawson was written in ink.

"Thank you, gentlemen this court will take a fifteen minute recess. Mr. Frederickson, Mr. Fitzgibbons will you and your team of lawyers please join me in my chambers."

The court clerk spoke after the judge tapped his wood gavel.

"All rise."

The judge and the lawyers stepped behind the big

wooden door leading to the judge's chambers. Seth and Jake looked at each other in a wondering glance. What was going on, why the conference. What had Fitzi shown the judge?

Chief Elm and Aubrey were worried about this wrinkle in the day's proceedings. Would their long-sought oversight be thrown to the curb again? His concern was showing, Elm closed his eyes and began his inner Thanksgiving Address.

What had seemed to be forty minutes of angst was only a little more than five minutes before the two teams of legal wizardry stepped from the judge's chambers. Both teams walked to their positions and stood.

"All Rise, the First District of Northern New York is now in session."

Judge McNally walked behind the bench and sat. The lawyers and those attending today's court session took their seats. Something had transpired in those five minutes. Something monumental Seth felt it. Checkmark for Fitzi.

Judge McNally adjusted his notes, he looked to his left to Niles, Fitzi and Walli. Then he looked to his right to the four government lawyers and then he looked directly at Seth. It unnerved Seth somewhat. Why was the judge looking at me Seth pondered.

"Ladies and gentlemen, Mr. Gunderson sir. This court has jurisdiction over many items relative to the Constitution of the United States and the laws of this nation. For over two hundred and twenty eight years the First District of New York, being the first federal court in the United States has heard many cases related to the rights of the indigenous people here in America."

He paused for a moment looking again across those assembled in his court.

"This court has been asked to affirm that the Two Row Wampum, The Treaty of Fort Stanwix and others exist. And that in these treaties existing that the indigenous people and nations have oversight of their territorial lands."

Judge McNally paused again. Seth noted a little tell from the judge. A smile, sort of. Checkmark for Niles.

"This court acknowledges that the Treaties between the United States of America and the Haudenosaunee exist and have so since their ratification by the Senate two thirds majority. This court in this acknowledgement however also has no jurisdiction on the oversight question brought before this Court. Therefore, while this court affirms the treaties, it does not have jurisdiction to rule in the regard of that requested oversight. That question is for a court higher than mine. This court rules that the treaties between the Haudenosaunee and the United States exist and that the question for oversight is one for the courts in Washington, DC."

Seth and Jake looked at each other in a surprised quiet joy. Had the judge just ruled the treaties were real? Did Niles just win? Elm and Aubrey held hands as the judges gavel struck down.

"All rise."

Judge Nolan McNally rose and walked through the open door to his chambers. He had ruled correctly on the treaties, and he had passed on the oversight. McNally was relieved. Kitty's and a Guinness were in order.

The Full House

The world in Northern Michigan was in full bloom. Memorial Day was the next week, and summers warmth was creeping up the shores of Lake Michigan. Seth was readying the pub for the summer rush that always began with the trickle of summer residents opening their lake cottages around Petosky.

Niles had called last night and conveyed that Fitzi wanted to do a conference call or some ZOOM thing with he and Seth. Niles wasn't adept to technology other than his flip phone and cable television. Seth told him to stop over in the morning and they could make the ZOOM call from the pub on his laptop.

He heard the old Coastie enter the back bar as Seth was wiping down the old mahogany planked bar. Niles slid in through the kitchen service door and sat on his stool. Seth had the two coffee cups filled with fresh brew as he poured in the traditional morning shot of warmth from Niles' favorite bottle behind the bar. This was the drink, coffee and a splash of spirits that Niles and Archie had shared a hundred times in the mornings when a decision was pending.

Niles put the steaming cup of coffee to his lips with both hands and sipped the top off. "We have a scheduled court date in DC. That's what Fitzi wants to talk about on the call."

Jake took his first sip. The warmth and the spirits awakened his big frame. He leaned back with his arms raised and stretched like a big bear in the north woods.

"What's the date, how many days?" Seth yawned.

Niles explained that Fitzi needed us in DC for four days. Chief Elm, Aubrey and Jake too. Fitzi was going to detail the arguments he would raise to Seth and Niles from their point or perspective. "June 3rd through the 7th. He has a hotel all lined up at a decent rate for everyone."

Seth took out his daily planner and noted the 2nd through the 8th for his travel.

"How's little Margaret Grace doing? What she's four

months now?" Niles asked. Seth grinned a big wide smile, he had a little princess now. Jakey was almost four years and eight months old; he was already the big brother of his little sister. She made him laugh. "She's good Niles. She has Alva's deep brown eyes and Betsy smile and beauty. I am a lucky man, yes sir in more ways than I could ever had imagined."

Seth took another sip. He turned the TV on so Niles could watch MASH, his favorite show. Seth went over to his office and grabbed his laptop. After a few minutes of logging in and navigating the email prompt for ZOOM the two waited for Fitzi to open the call. This kind of communication dazzled and overwhelmed Niles. He looked at the laptop and saw Fitzi and his face. Fitzi chuckled, "You need a shave old man." Niles fired back, "Cut the crap you old son of bitch I am paying you for this time so don't waste mine…" All three men laughed with Niles comeback.

The lawyer rolled out his case and the tactics and strategies he was going to use in court before the justices. Walli had nailed down all the constitutional legal precedents and documents which solidify the position of stewardship.

"So do we proceed gentlemen?"

Niles looked at Seth and nodded. "What's this going to cost?"

Fitzi said, "Only charging you for the court time old man. That work for you?"

Seth thanked him for his passion and commitment to this endeavor. Niles was paying Walli in cash too. That was the side joke.

Niles asked where they were staying in DC. "The Dubliner, it's a great hotel with a good bar and restaurant. We can do the court thing, and all stay in one place."

See you on the 2nd Seth finished the call.

Two weeks later Seth and Niles boarded a plane from Pellston Airport for Detroit and then a direct flight to Reagan International Airport in Washington, DC. They boarded the Pellston flight at 07:10 and were airborne by 07:20. Seth had grabbed the window seat. As the small jet lifted off the east end of the runway Seth looked down and saw Archie's grave. He knew it well as the former Marine would often drive through the little cemetery and talked to Archie about "things."

Seth whispered to himself, "Semper Fi old man, Semper Fi." He smiled as knew Archie was with him on this new journey to Washington. Archie was always with him.

The flight was unencumbered by any delays or issues, and they arrived in Washington fifteen minutes ahead of the 11:20 am scheduled time. When they went through the concourse exit there was Fitzi standing by the luggage belt. He had bags to get. Niles and Seth had traveled with a small suitcase and Seth had his Marine rucksack. Seth helped Fitzi with his baggage thinking what's this guy bringing to court?

Fitzi had arranged for a car service to pick them up and take them to the Dubliner Pub & Hotel. It was a short ten-minute ride. The Dubliner was a beautiful old-style pub with a deep Irish theme and history. It was owned by one of the Kelly boys from Syracuse. Fitzi had met the owner Denny Kelly back when he was doing lobbying work for his firm here in DC. They had shared a few Cubans on the upper porch above the front entrance telling stories. Denny had given him a special rate for Niles, Seth, Walli and Fitzi. Dennis Kelly had comped the three rooms for the representatives from Onondaga. His father had known Chief Elm's father and uncles from his youth growing up in the Salt City of Syracuse, New York.

When the car service pulled up in front of the hotel Niles smiled. There was a warmth or sense of energy he felt as the doorman opened his door. Niles and Seth each grabbed their bag as the bellman removed Fitzi's luggage from the trunk. Fitzi handed the driver a twenty and turned to see Denny smiling at the beautiful wide wooden doors. The proprietor welcomed his old friend and the new guests staying for the duration of the court proceedings.

The three travel weary men followed Denny into the lobby as the bellman headed for the elevator. He already knew which room was Fitzi's. Seth and Niles turned to go to the hotel main desk and Denny waved them on. "You boys are checked in." Fitzi had a special rate. "I have you on the same floor as Mrs. Owltree." Chief Elm and Chief Owltree. When the elevator opened, they were on the executive floor of the historic hotel. This was the floor the Irish Prime Minister and other important guests visiting the United States capital resided during their stays. Kelly knew that Chief Elm was a world leader as the Tadodaho of the Haudenosaunee Six Nations. The Tadodaho is the supreme leader of Six Nation Grand Council and the spiritual leader of the Confederacy.

As the three new arrivals settled into their respective suites Denny joined Fitzi in his. Fitzi tipped the bellman as Denny poured them both some of his special reserve Irish Whiskey. A three finger pour...

"So, tell me Fitz, how the hell did you get a court date at the Supreme Court?"

"That former Marine and his godfather Niles are a pretty formidable pair. Seth might be six foot eight and still wearing his tight Marine style haircut, but that kid is a leader and a brilliant man. He could be president of the United States. The kid is a pub owner like you, second generation too." Denny's father had opened an Irish pub in the Tipperary Hill neighborhood of Syracuse called Kelly's. It was a true Irish pub. That upbringing had driven Denny to his career in hospitality that led to his owning the Dubliner.

"I have a lunch set up for you all in the executive dining room on the third floor. We can go down once we finish our welcome beverage."

Fitzi briefed Kelly on the discovery that Seth had found in the Constitution and how Niles was his client paying him $9.87 per hour. Denny Kelly knew his friend told him he was working for that small fee. Fitzgibbons would be hard to take down in the courtroom. He was a bear of a barrister and one damn good lawyer.

The lunch was a bounty of fresh seafood, fruits and vegetables. Chief Elm had asked that they visit the National Museum of the American Indian. He had been at the museum grand opening but did not have the time to stroll through the exhibits. He wanted to spend some time walking and learning what was presented. Kelly had reserved the hotels Mercedes Sprinter Passenger Van for the week as transportation for the team of lawyers, the old Coastie, Seth and the Onondaga Delegation.

The driver was Charlie Applegate, he was a retired FBI veteran and former US Army Special Forces member. Applegate wore a suit that hid the Glock 19M he carried. Charlie had been the senior agent in charge of the FBI's shooting and gun range for his last eight years of service. There was no security threat with this group of guests, but Kelly knew if there ever were, his guests would be protected and safe from harm.

Aubrey was overwhelmed by the generosity and welcoming nature of Dennis Kelly. He had a warm character and engaging personality that brought a feeling of visiting an old friend. Chief Elm was overwhelmed by the traffic and buzz of the United States Capital. It was a short drive of only nine minutes, the old chief thankfully thought.

When they arrived at the museum there was a small delegation of the museum staff waiting for the lawyers and the Onondaga Leaders. Denny Kelly joined them with intrigue. Aubrey Owltree was the clan mother of clan mothers in their sovereign lands.

This afternoon Chief Elm and Aubrey would be leading the tour of the exhibits and would tell the stories of their people and all of Turtle Island original residents. Aubrey would explain the principle of no one owning the land and that the ultimate destiny for her people and the American people is to find the peace between their nations and peace with Mother Earth.

As they walked up to the museum steps Elm offered a small lighting of tobacco which is in tribute and honor of the Creator. The offering also brings purification to those who witness this ancient offering. Then Chief Elm asked Seth to give the Thanksgiving Address, which he did mostly in English. Seth asked Jake to finish in the Onondaga language.

There was no media, Chief Elm had asked for none as

he was just visiting the museum and here to support his friend Niles. A world leader was visiting Washington, DC and no one knew. There would be time for CBS, NBC, CNN, ABC, and the other world news organizations to know that the Onondaga Nation was in town. For now, stealth was the strongest position until Fitzi stood before the Supreme Court on Niles' behalf.

First Volley

The Supreme Court of the United States is the most reverent space of justice in American. The court was the third leg of the stool modern democracy rests on. The other two being the executive branch and the congress. Niles had sued all three branches of his government. This was to be a historic moment in the court, a challenge that might change the direction of America's future in respect to native rights over original aboriginal lands.

As the passenger van approached the huge building located behind the US Capital Building Niles began to get nervous as he noticed the satellite trucks and small tented positions of the news media. There was no hiding now. The time of stealth had ended. Fitzi had briefed every one of the gaggle of press that would be present and to just smile and follow him with no comment from anyone in the group, now or until he won.

Fitzi was followed by Walli and then Niles with Chief Elm and Aubrey walking with Seth on one side and Jake on the other. As they entered the court building through the side door the press corps began yelling questions at Niles and the leaders of the Six Nations.

"Mr. Gunderson, why are you suing your own country to benefit the Indians?" Another yelled, "What to do wish to accomplish at the Supreme Court?"

Fitzi winked at Seth and Niles as he stepped aside and walked over to the assemblage of press.

"Thank you for your questions. My client believes in the constitution of the United States, he supports our president, the congress and the courts. Mr. Gunderson is a retired history teacher and retired town judge from Walloon, Michigan. He brought this action to ensure the citizens of this country, as well as the Onondaga's and Six Nations future is secured relative to the land, nature, the environment. And future for this and the next seven generations. As his lawyer I can tell you he appreciates the court allowing his argument and belief in what is lawful, and right to be adhered to. Thank you."

Twenty minutes later after passing through the courts security system and magnetometers that scan for weapons and contraband, Chief Elm, Mrs. Owltree, Jake and Seth entered the courtroom. It was a court like no other in the land of the United States. Chief Elm took in a deep breath and slowly let the moment envelop him. Elm was nervous, this was where his people had always hoped to be. Before the colonialists, supreme judges. The Six Nations had a similar setting with wooden benches in the longhouse at Onondaga, where all the nations met on issues relative to the confederacy of indigenous Six Nations. The Onondaga Nation were the Fire Keepers, the home of the central government of the Six Nations. Today, Elm, Aubrey Owltree and her son Jake Owltree were merely spectators with a front row seat. The fate of their oversight of the ancestral lands was at stake.

Chief Elm and Aubrey sat in the rear on the right side of the gallery in the court behind Niles and the two legal warriors representing the old Coastie. Seth was seated across on the left on the US side of the court. Seth bowed his head and began saying the Thanksgiving Address in his head, Jake did the same. Both Chief Elm and Aubrey could almost hear the two brothers in their minds giving thanks and praise to the Creator. Aubrey smiled; she was not the nervous type.

It was several minutes as the government lawyers, Fitzi and Walli were settled. And then the moment arrived.

"All rise… The Supreme Court of the United States of America is now in session. Please remain standing until all the justices are seated."

The nine Justices of the United States Supreme Court all entered the courtroom and demonstrated the long tradition of the "Judicial Handshake" where each justice shakes the hand of the other eight justices signaling that the differences of opinion on this United States Supreme Court should not override the overall purpose and responsibility of the court to uphold the laws of the United States Constitution. They stepped to their seats all nodding to the clerk and those assembled. The eight judges of the lands highest court sat down looking out over the gallery and lawyers as the ninth, the Chief Justice said, "Please be seated everyone."

The Chief Justice, Horatio J. Jones IV, was in his seventeenth year on the Supreme Court. He had been a Federal Judge in his home state of New Hampshire, served as a State Supreme Court Judge and prior was a constitutional lawyer and Judge Advocate General in the United States Marines. Judge Jones had attended the United States Navel Academy where he was a linebacker on the same team as Rodger Staubach, whose professional career was as one of the best quarterbacks of all time. Staubach and Jones were friends, they were beyond friends, they were football brothers.

Seth had read his bio on the courts website and was impressed, and the others as well. He two had served two plus tours in the Marine Corp and Naval legal system. With a degree in history, political science and a major in mechanical engineering Horatio "Rat" Jones as his Marine buddies had called him was a learned man. He attended the Yale Law School for his Juris Doctorate Law Degree at the urging of his father's friend Augustus Schall whose tenure as a Federal Judge in New Hampshire was historic for adhering to the Constitution of the United States. To the letter and intent of the frames of this document for democracy.

Fitzi and Walli had done all the pre-trail submissions, they had presented written arguments, a replica of the Two Row Wampum, The Friendship Belt, the Silver Chain and the Everett Report. Evidence between the government lawyers and Niles two-man team had transpired in the traditional old lawyer way with dignity and that lawyer gruffness of competitors.

The formal introduction of the legal representatives was next and noted by the courteous smiles exchanged. Seth could see Fitzi' feathers plum like that of a male peacock as he smiled and tilted his head down to the six barristers at the opposing table. And the stout Irish Chicago lawyer actually wore a male peacock tie on today in the court. The government's lawyers' ties were red and blue. Seth took out his steno pad and noted one check for Fitzi. He would keep the score on who won what discussion or moment whether by words or a peacock tie.

Chief Judge Jones rolled through the courts agenda for the morning and the rules he sternly adhered to. Seth noticed the judge at times sheepishly glancing back at him. When Jones glanced at Seth the third time he nodded and smiled at the Chief Judge whose steadfastness on the bench was uneased by Seth's nod. No one saw it but Seth. In his steno pad he had written with a line underneath; Fitzi, Government, Court and then toward the bottom he wrote Seth. When anyone of these four, primarily the original three, won a moment he would pencil in a checkmark under the name. So far it was one check for Fitzi and one for Seth.

A court room can be laborious and boring to most folks. A little of this and a little of that in words exchanged, arguments made, objections if needed and the occasional exchange of humor.

About an hour into the hearing one of the justices asked Fitzi if the plaintiff would answer several of her questions. Judge Caroline Judith Beccerria, was a New Yorker from Brooklyn. She had been a democratic when she was the ADA in Queens prior to running for city, then the state court and eventually appointed to the Supreme Court Bench by President Bill Clinton.

Fitzi huddled next to Niles whispering in his ear. Niles smiled and let out a little chuckle. Seth was smiling too, he knew Fitzi was telling his godfather another one of his dirty jokes. The court room stillness was broken when Niles looked at his two lawyers and the nine justices and said, "Mam, I mean your honor, Judge Beccerria I would be honored to answer any questions you or the other justices would like me too."

Niles in his simple demeanor with the ease of his smooth whiskey voice had won a moment. Check mark for both Niles and Fitzi. So far on his pad Seth had noted six checks for the government, five for the judges, four for Fitzi, one for himself and two for Niles. The old man was working the nine heads of America's top court and they had no clue. Niles was not Peter Falk in the television series "Columbo", however his soothing rhythm, his unbeknownst knowledge of the laws, of early American history, the Everett Report and his innate ability to answer the questions and reply with an answer that questioned the question was brilliant.

After Judge Beccerria, three other Justices asked questions related to his reasoning and intent for his filing. The old teacher, firefighter, local town judge and former Coastie had drawn in the nine, he had answered the inquiries as if he himself were one of the nine. Chief Elm looked over at Seth and nodded. Seth smiled and put his clenched fist above his heart. He loved Niles as he loved his father and grandfather.

Niles put down seven checks on the note pad. One for each of the Justices that he felt Niles had won over.

Then Chief Justice Jones asked Niles if he had anything left to add.

"Mr. Gunderson, I am impressed with your argument

and more so with you sir for your belief in our laws, our manner of dealing justice and more so for your service as a United States Coast Guardsman, a teacher, a first responder and a local judge in your town and community. You sir are and represent what is truly dear and most cherished in our country. A patriot. One last question sir, if I may…"

"Of course, your honor, please ask whatever you would like."

The Chief Judge looked out across the court glancing at the back where Chief Elm, Aubrey and Jake were seated and then he paused looking directly at Seth.

Seth was a little unnerved by that small but powerful moment. He put two checks under the judges list.

"As a former town judge and history teacher, if you would please explain to the court your argument for giving the Onondaga Nation a level of oversight of their ancestral lands? And if you would sir please speak as if you were one of the nine members of this court here today. Most of us started our journey in the court system, in a small court room like you did during your tenure in Walloon Lake and Petosky Michigan."

Niles was good, but he never thought this one through.

Never imagined ever being a Justice on the Supreme Court of the United States of America. Seth was a little unnerved by the question and Chief Elm noted it.

Niles was not. He took three deep breaths, he smiled at the nine members of the court. He looked at the governments six lawyers, he turned and looked at Mrs. Owltree, Jake and Chief Elm. And he looked at Seth and with his head turned away from the judges he winked. Only Seth saw it. To everyone in the court room it looked like the old man was just doing what old men do. The little eye flutter to everyone signaled to Seth that his godfather was about to make his case.

"Chief Justice Jones and your fellow justices. Like you I took an oath to," he raised his right hand.

"I do solemnly swear (or affirm) that I will faithfully execute the office as a Coastguards Man, teacher or local town judge, and will to the best of my ability, preserve, protect and defend the Constitution of the United States."

Niles lowered his right hand and spoke further.

"Sir it was my duty, my sworn duty to adhere to the laws of our nation, to the rights of men and women, and to defend those that may need defending. Our laws

Article II, Section 2 of the United States Constitution states."

Niles pulled his tattered old worn copy of the Constitution out and read aloud Article II, Section 2 to the court room.

"the President shall have Power, by and with the Advice and Consent of the Senate to make Treaties, provided two thirds of the Senators present concur."

He went on…

"The Federal Court in New York referred my complaint, here after that court affirmed that the Treaty of Fort Stanwix was still an active agreement. That, this Treaty, that the Two Row Wampum and others exist between the Six Nations and the United States of America. The question that is brought before the honored court is simple. If the government admits and accepts that the Treaty is valid, it exists and has never been un-ratified then to what level of oversight does that Treaty provide the Six Nations over all the lands included in that Treaty."

"The Onondagas do not want to take land from any landowner in their ancestral homelands. In the land of the Onondaga and the Six Nations it is recognized that no one owns the land. That you live on the land, you farm it, you harvest berries and venison, you fish the streams for trout and salmon in the fall. But you don't own the land. More importantly in Onondaga it is said that all decisions made should be inconsideration of the Seventh Generation. You cherish the resources the planet and Creator have provided. You thank nature every day for the bounties it provides for sustenance and medicines."

Niles stopped and took a sip of water. He was almost ninety-six now.

"We share the same river, the same farmland now as the Two Row Wampum details without words. We breathe the same air, and we raise our families. This decision before the Supreme Court is about the law of the land and in the end, it is about the integrity of the United States of America as the land of the FREE and the home of the Brave. If we as a nation disavow the core values of democracy; Life, Liberty, and the pursuit of Happiness as declared in the Declaration of Independence, in this case, well then, we all turn our backs on freedom. You asked me what or why I brought this action. For peace across our shared lands, for strong oversight on our resources so that in Seven Generation your children's, children's, children's future as well as the democratic republic we live on, in America as we call it, or Great Turtle Island as the Onondaga's call this land; will be flourishing and the people living their lives in peace."

He paused; the old man was weakening with the old age of old age. Ninety-six-years-old and Niles could fight like a teenager, thought Seth. He worried for his godfathers health.

Niles finished the answer to the question of the Chief Judge.

"Chief Justice Jones, if I were seated to your right or left, I would have written down the following on a note pad and slid it over to you discretely. Four words sir; It's time for a parlay. I guess that's five words. Why not let the Onondaga Nation choose a representative and the United States choose a representative and we work it out? Compromise, if the President concurs, he sends it to the Senate for a vote and hopefully two-thirds of the Senate ratifies and affirms the new agreement."

Niles, being a judge himself knew that the Supreme Court wished he had never filed, never won in the Federal Courts of New York. But he did. Niles was giving the court a way out of making the decision. He was suggesting that the court throw it back to the Executive Branch of the United States Government and let them work it out.

There was silence in the court as Niles sat down.

Seth took his pencil and drew a big W on the page. Niles had won, he felt.

Justice Jones looked to his right and then to his left. He repeated that motion once more.

"Mr. Gunderson, you sir would make a fine Justice of the Supreme Court. Your words make a good argument for the Executive, our President to parlay as you say and see if we can find common ground."

Chief Elm and Aubrey grasped each other's hand. Seth sat in the back un-waivered by the moment. He knew something good was brewing in the court.

"I believe your argument is true and genuine Mr. Gunderson. And this court will adjourn until tomorrow morning to consider all you have said."

Judge Jones smiled at the court and then smiled at Seth.

"This court is adjourned until tomorrow at 9:30 am."

"All rise, the Supreme Court of the United States is now adjourned."

New Commission

When the court room was empty. Niles, Walli and Fitzi strolled to the back and sat next to Chief Elm and Aubrey. Jake was chatting with Seth across the aisle. There was a sense of victory, but not a feeling of winning. Nothing had been won yet.

As the eight were awaiting a text to indicate the Dubliner Courtesy van was at the rear door of the Courthouse a clerk entered the courtroom and asked to speak with Mr. Longfield. Seth waved his right hand and the young woman walked over.

"Mr. Longfield?"

"Yes," Seth answered.

"Would you please come with me sir? The Chief Justice wants a word with you."

A little stunned, Seth nodded, he looked at Elm, Aubrey, Jake and Niles. Niles winked at him again with his left eye, with that Niles patented wink.

"Sure, should my friends wait?"

"No sir, the Chief Justice will give you a ride back to your hotel."

Seth nodded and gave Jake a pat on the back. "Keep an eye on Niles please, he looks a little worn out."

Jake winked his left eye. The code was left, YES and when you wink your right eye, NO.

Three minutes later Seth was ushered into the large wood panel office of the Chief Justice of the United States Supreme Court. It was an overwhelming moment, one that was truly giving Seth a feeling of pride mixed with a little bit of fear. He was sweating and felt unsure of the moment. The Chief Justice rose from his side chair by the window looking out at the Capital, the National Mall and in the distance the Lincoln and Jefferson Memorials and finally the Washington Monument.

Jones extended his hand to shake Seth's.

"Mr. Longfield, pleasure to meet a fellow Marine. Horatio J. Jones the IV. My friends call me Rat. Please join me here and let's chat a little. May I call you Seth sir? You can call me Rat Seth..."

"Seth is fine Sir, although Sir you out rank me in the Marines. Do you mind if I call you Sir, Sir?"

Jones laughed out loud, a big brown bear of a laugh.

"Seth, Sir, Sir is a little to formal. Just sir if that makes you comfortable."

"Thank you, Sir." Seth replied as he sat with a cautious grin.

"I have some lemonade and Arizona Green Tea with Honey. I call it a Winnie Palmer after Arnie's first wife. Love an Arnold Palmer. Had to switch to the green tea because of Kidney Stones. Black Tea, peanut butter, chocolate, they give me kidney stones you could break a stained-glass church window with." He went on that the green tea version did not cause stones, and it was better for you than black tea.

"Where did you serve Seth? How's life after two active tours?"

"Two tours and two years Sir. I was on a special team. Chief Owltree was my squad leader. We were together since Basic, through special ops training and then deployed over twelve missions together."

"Sounds like you two are brothers?"

"Yes Sir, all Marines are brothers."

"Yes, we are Seth."

Seth's mouth was as dry as the Afghan desert. He raised the glass of ice and the cold Winnie Palmer and poured it down in one slow long gulp. When he put his glass back on the side table Jones filled it again. Seth took out a fresh pressed white hankie and wipe his brow of the sweat.

"Your godfather must have been a fair and just judge in his days serving on the bench. His argument was a good one today. He would be a good member of this court."

Seth leaned forward.

"Sir, he is a good and just man. Niles and my grandfather were like brothers. He has always been protective of me. Honestly, I would have sued the state and federal government, but he said no. That I should sit in the courts and listen. That I should read the treaties and the Constitution thoroughly. And besides all that he might be the smartest old Coastie on the Planet. My godfather gave you folks an out today."

Jones was taken aback for a moment by Seth's statement. And then smiled.

"Son, that old man took the monkey off our backs today. Well, I should say the Federal Court in New York affirmed the Treaty of Fort Stanwix. This court will not argue with that ruling. But it's the executives job to make treaties not the courts."

Jones paused. "However, the court does have its say on how things move forward. I called the President after our session. I asked that you be appointed to the role of Special Master to the court and the executive branch. Now you can decline if you want to, however your President will be asking you to serve if you decline my request. And it's hard to decline a direct order from your President as a Marine."

"It is Sir, although, ummm, as a retired Marine I could decline based on my personal responsibility as a father and business owner."

"Yes, yes you could as a retired Marine. However, Seth Longfield, you have been re-activated for this special mission by the President of the United States of America. Oh, and you are now a Lt. Colonel in the United States Marine Corp."

Seth was stunned, for just a moment. And then he felt it. He felt the warmth of Archie envelop his frame and soul. He stood and snapped to attention and saluted the Chief Justice.

"Lt. Colonel Longfield reporting for duty Sir."

Jones was impressed. The Chief Justice of the Supreme Court rose and saluted Seth. He was more than impressed, Chief Justice Jones was honored and proud to be a Marine.

"Semper Fi, LT Colonel, Sempre Fi", Jones said as he to stood returning the salute.

The Chief Justice and Seth settled into their cushioned wood armchairs. These were the chairs from the Chief Justices office that have been in this office for over one hundred years. There was history in these comfy seats and history was about to be born again.

Jones asked Seth to sit for a moment and think through the appointment, he had to make a phone call.

"Gerard, thank you for taking me up on my idea. Yes sir, yes sir. I will tell Shelly you send her your regards. She is up in New Hampshire with our new grand baby. Hannah J Jones, sir."

Jones handed the phone to Seth. "It's the President, he wants to speak to you."

Seth's hands began to quiver ever so lightly as he took

the phone from Rat Jones. Gerard Foster Lawson was the forty sixth president of the United States. A democratic from Virginia, he was a moderate for a democrat.

"Lt. Colonel, President Lawson here son. Listen Rat tells me you're the man to work this situation out. I appreciate you taking on this task. Vice President Gardner will be my liaison, and as President of the Senate his role is take back whatever you and our government and the Onondaga Nation come to terms with. The VP will need to roll up sixty-six senators to approve any changes or new understandings for amending the treaty. The VP and the Secretaries of the Interior and Health and Human Services as well as the Secretary of State will be negotiating on our behalf. Chief Elm and the Onondagas can choose up to four members as well. As Special Master in these meetings you are the person in charge. It is your mission, your objective to find common ground, a common shared interest based on our shared values. It is with this intention that I trust you with son."

"Yes Sir" Seth automatically stood up on instinct.

"Yes Sir, I will Sir. Thank you Sincerely, I won't let you down Mr. President."

"That is why you were chosen Mr. Longfield. My

grandkids future and yours and that other Marine, Sft. Sgt. Owltree kids and grandkids depend on it. This is not about the land and who owns what, it is about how we deal with caring for it and each other." The President paused.

"Thank you, Seth, I have to run. Have a call scheduled with my nine-year-old grandson. He's learning to baseball and always has questions. Be well and God Bless you son, and God Bless America."

Seth stood there motionless for a few seconds as the line went dead.

"He hung up on you didn't he. He always does before you can wish him well. Just his thing I guess."

Jones had some questions for Seth.

"So, how's the fishing up there in Northern Michigan? I've read the Nick Adams stories every summer on vacation. I still love reading about Hemingway fishing the streams of Walloon Lake and Indian River."

Jones went on.

"It's excellent Sir. You will have to come up some summer and I will take you to some of my favorite little holes for rainbows or in the fall for the Salmon runs. Do you like fried perch and fresh walleye?"

"Do I ever Seth. I will join someday or weekend soon."

The Chief Justice called his secretary and told her to get his car ready for him to take Seth back to the Dubliner. It was an amazing day for a bar keep from Northern Michigan.

Seth texted Jake and told him he would be on his way back soon. The ensemble from Onondaga and Northern Michigan were scheduled to visit the Vietnam Veterans Memorial Wall of Honor, the Three Service Men's Statue and the Vietnam Women's Memorial. Chief Elm had a brother whose name was on the Wall as did Aubrey. Aubrey also had a cousin who served as a nurse who was killed in a forward MASH unit.

Jake texted back. "we r onway to wall nw. can you get ride over???."

Seth pondered asking if it was appropriate to ask the Chief Justice to drop him off by the Wall. The old judge noticed the slight frown on Seth's face.

"Something on your mind Seth?"

Seth was impressed, "Yes Sir, do you mind dropping off by the Vietnam Memorial Sir. Chief Elm and Mrs. Owltree are heading there now to look for their relatives who both perished in Nam."

"Anywhere you want Seth."

Walking the Wall

The motorcade of the Chief Justice was not as ceremonial as the President's caravan. It was still impressive. Two Capital motorcycles at the front and two at the rear. The first vehicle was a huge GMC Yukon followed by another with the Chief Justice riding in the second Yukon and the third tight behind Jones' armored vehicle was a large Cadillac that had six former Marine Special Forces members locked and loaded to deflect any possible assault on the Chief Justice.

Seth was impressed with the fire power and the technical aspects of moving the CJOTUS around the capital of the United States. It had only been twenty minutes since his call with the President. Seth's mind had been racing.

"Sir, may I ask you a question and also a small request?"

"Certainly, Seth."

"Well,", scratching his neck on the right side. "What exactly do I do sir? I mean the VP is in the room, the secretaries, the Onondaga's. Who are part of my family now, as you well know. How do I know what right sir is, for all of us?"

The Chief Justice smiled. "Seth you are trained as a Marine to do the right thing. You know in your heart and in your oath to the Constitution what is right. You just have to listen to what is possible and then let others know that vision."

"What's your request Seth?"

"May I call you sir; I mean if I need some guidance on the law or something?"

"Yes son, anytime night or day. Here is my personal cell number. Anytime you need to, that's an order." Jones laughed as he handed Seth his simple white card with his name on it. Nothing else. Just Horatio J. Jones IV and the number.

Seth looked at the card. "May I ask what the J stands for sir?"

"My Grandmother got to choose my middle name. She was a pretty creative woman; her grandfather was the first federal judge in New Hampshire after the Revolution."

"So, your middle name is after his name then?"

"No she was a wise woman who could see I guess, see into the future." Horatio Justice Jones the IV. Although only you and my wife now know what the J stands for. The birth certificate only had J as the middle name like my father, grandfather, great-grandfather and his father.

"That's cool…" Seth was smiling.

"John, pull up into the little driveway by the wall please. We are gonna drop you off as close as possible."

The motorcade pulled up to the edge of the historic National Mall adjacent to the Vietnam Memorial. CJOTUS thanked Seth for taking on this mission. Seth nodded and stuck out his right hand. The two men shook hands as only two Marine's sharing that moment before an important mission.

"God Bless Seth, and Semper Fi son." The two exchanged a salute.

Seth stepped out of the vehicle as the door was opened by one of the security team. He waved back at the open door and trotted off on his journey. First to The Wall and then to his duty.

It was only three minutes until he saw Chief Elm and Aubrey, they were tracing a name off the wall on paper to take back to the Nation. Jake was off in the distance kneeling and praying. Seth began to feel that engulfing emotion of brotherly love for those lost souls. He stopped and shuttered for a moment. To much was happening. He knew this day would come, however somehow the emotion of The Wall was overwhelming his strong core.

He closed his eyes and thought of his beautiful wife and best friend, his two children and that eased his soul. He opened his eyes and scanned further across the landscape surrounding the wall. And then he saw Niles, just sitting on a bench in the shade. The old Coastie was resting his aged bones. Niles had his handkerchief out and was wiping his eyes.

Seth slowly strode over and sat next to his godfather.

"You OK Niles? You need some water?"

Niles nodded, "Yeah, the damn pollen is up and has my eyes watering."

Seth reached into his small shoulder bag and pulled out a water bottle, handing it to Niles.

"Yes, Seth I am ok. Just a little tired with the day's

activities and seeing this Wall. When does war stop son, when the hell does war stop?"

Niles put his hand on Seth's left knee.

"How bout you kid. How did the unexpected meet and greet go with the Chief Justice?"

Seth detailed the meeting, the judge's request. His conversation with the President and his new commission. He smiled and chuckled. "Seems you did such a good job, the court was thankful. And both you and Chief Elm told me I was to be the Peace Maker. And now I am the Special Master Peace Maker…"

They both broke out in a light but cheerful laugh.

Seth's phone vibrated; he answered the Restricted Number.

"Yes, thank you, yes. I'll hold yes."

Looking at Niles he grinned and mouthed, "Game On!"

Rule of the Day

The group arrived back at the Dubliner Hotel around 4:30 pm and were dropped off at the back loading dock. The media was planted out front with their satellite trucks, their little white tents to keep them shaded and dry if DC received a late afternoon shower.

The Onondaga's were a little overwhelmed with the attention. Niles shrugged them off as a bunch of talking knuckleheads.

Seth was scanning the crowd for threats or other unintended consequences; it was a natural behavior for a Marine. He had told Niles not to mention his new appointment and mission. Seth wanted to discuss it over dinner which was scheduled for 5:30 pm in the private dining room. Seth walked Niles to his room and helped him lay down on the soft king-size bed in his suite.

"Lay down and rest Niles. I will get you up for dinner, I just want you to be careful, you're gonna be ninety-seven in November and I need a hunting partner."

Seth slowly exited the room and went to his suite next door through the connecting French Doors.

He needed to make some notes and make a call or two to the hotel and State Department and VP. The hotel was first. He called Dennis Kelly who came up to his suite. Next was the State Department Under Secretary of Operations.

Seth detailed the agenda. Three days of meetings, starting promptly at 10:00 am with a lunch break at 12:30 pm and the remaining meeting going from 2:00 pm till 5:30 pm. Each department could have an aide and a stenographer attend the meeting with the Secretary of State, Secretary of Health and Human Services, and the Secretary of the Interior.

Then he delivered the location. The treaty discussion would take place at the Dubliner Hotel. Seth had arranged for the Hotel upper ballroom for the meetings. The building was a secure structure, and the State

Department could assign whatever security they deemed appropriate. He gave the under-Secretary of State Dennis Kelly's cell phone number. Then Seth dialed the office of the Vice President.

Seth was connected with the Vice Presidents Executive Assistant, Mary O'Conner and explained the meeting agenda. Then he expressed that the VP could attend when he wants based on his calendar. Mary told him to please hold the line.

Seconds later, the Vice President was on the line.

"Lt. Colonel Longfield, pleasure to take your call sir. I know we have a few meetings this week. How can I be of assistance.?"

"Thank you sir. I am honored to speak to you and to have been chosen by the President for this mission sir. Just paying you the courtesy sir, of informing your staff of our agenda and timetable. I told Ms. O'Conner that you are welcome to attend as your calendar allows you to."

The VP explained he would be there for the morning session every day and that he did have obligations scheduled in the afternoons that could and would be adjusted if needed. Seth sensed the Vice President was looking to distance himself from the solution and was most likely waiting to understand the political side of this attempt to reconcile over two hundred years of ignoring the treaties. He and President Lawson were in the beginning of their second term and this VP did not want anything hanging over him in two years when he announced his intention to run for the top job.

When the call ended Seth went and showered. After he had dried off, he looked in his closet for a pair of kakis and a fresh shirt. It was then he saw the two full-dress Marine Uniforms, the two everyday dress uniforms, the two shoes, belts, hats and the medals he had been awarded pinned to all of his clean and stiff pressed duds. He was a Marine again. It shook his sensitive soul a little with the battle scars and memories. And then emotion of the pride in the mission, the sense of duty to himself, his oath, his nation and most importantly his family.

His phone rang and it was Seth's bride. He needed her now more than ever, needed her calming sense of balance and unwavering love.

"Hi, how are my babies princess?"

"Jakey wants to say hello."

His young son yelled, "How is Washton Dad?"

Seth did his best not to tear up.

Double Down

Tuesday's dinner the night before had been a meal of Thanksgiving. Dennis Kelly's chef had prepared his signature corn and clam chowder. There were fresh shucked oysters from Wellfleet on Cape Cod. Fresh Boston Cod with a butter crumb cracker topping and two selections of meat. Fresh venison and a smoked brisket. Smoked veggies, salad, shrooms and dessert.

Seth was nervous about his mission in which failure for the Onondaga Nation and his own nation was not an option. Over the appetizers Seth detailed his conversation with the Chief Justice, the President and the Vice President. He asked Aubrey for her blessing and thanked her for her love. Niles and Chief Elm agreed that Niles would not settle until there was a certain level of official recognition and planning on the Onondaga and other nations oversight of land.

Seth had put Niles to bed and now was engaged in reading his notes of the varied court sessions, his study of the Constitution and the Treaties, all of them between the Six Nations and the United States of America.

He was tired, actually Seth was a little worn around the edges as his pen stroked the yellow note pad with agenda items for discussion tomorrow. It was not long before Seth dropped the pad and pen.

When he awoke Seth stepped over to the bed and flopped down. His mind began to engage on the mission. He needed another hour of sleep. The father and husband's mind raced for the mission and eased into him standing in his favorite stream above Walloon Lake on a fall morning. The water running down along the brook with the crispness of winter creeping in. He was after that fat rainbow trout. The fall season was his favorite to be afield immersed in the natural world. The smell of the forest and leaves falling. He breathed in deeply. Ahhhhhh. The occasional group of does striding by. That illusive buck he would hunt in a month with his crossbow chasing his next female.

Seth was asleep.

When he awoke Seth totaled up his hours sleeping 5.75 and 1.5. Seven hours was a good recharge for his inner spirit. The next week would be in many ways the most important days in his life and the history of the Onondaga and Six Nations, and his nation.

Seth needed to get some physical stress blown off. He grabbed his Nike's, slid on a pair of running shorts and one of the new USMC tee shirts and stepped into the hallway. A Marine sentry snapped to attention startling Seth.

"Marine, may I ask what you are doing outside my room?" Seth showed him his new shiny dog tags.

"Yes sir. Sgt. Oscar Davis sir. I am assigned to you as your aide and well sir, also security sir. We have three Marines assigned to the detail sir."

"Well thank you Sgt."

"Yes sir, Lt. Colonel sir."

"I am going for a little run and walk soldier. I am requesting you stand your post here and keep an eye on Mr. Gunderson in case he needs something."

Seth turned and stepped to the stairway and down he

went. Sgt. Davis radioed the security team in the lobby that Seth was on the way down.

Seth knew there would be a security team awaiting his entering the lobby from the stairs. He needed to be alone. After quick stepping the stairs for three floors he ducked out on the fourth floor and made a quick turn to the Service Elevator and hit the button for the laundry and rear dock area.

When the elevator door opened, he headed directly for the dock. Two long strides down the steps and he was off running. Well trotting was more the pace. Seth's huge frame popped out in front of the Dubliner, and he turned right. It was 0514 and the sun was not yet above the horizon. He was hoping that the media would not recognize him. They did not.

Seth was free. The hot humid air of Washington, DC enveloped his body by the end of the first block and the sweat started to make its way out his pores. His heartbeat increased as his brow began to slightly sweat. The pent-up physical stress of the last week was boiling out his pours as he turned left covering another block and turned left again. Seth glanced back over his shoulder; he was alone. Gliding along now with the coolness of the morning flowing over his now full body sweat. He could see the Capital ahead four blocks, then three, then one block to go. He was in full stride now and hurdled the concrete barrier. Seth continued on another one hundred fifty yards and pulled up standing in the shadow of the United States Capital Building. His hands on his knees breathing deeply, Seth dropped to one knee and started to pray. Giving the Sign of the Cross he prayed for his family, for the Onondaga's, for Niles, for the members attending today's session, for the air he was breathing and the birds singing their morning symphony. Seth felt peace, he felt at ease.

It was then he heard the footsteps off to his left side. Seth rose and turned slowly around.

"Lt. Colonel Longfield? Sir, ummm, you are in a restricted area sir. I need you to come with me sir. The supervisor over there needs to speak with you sir."

Seth looked to his right and saw a Capital Police Officer waiving him over. Seth saluted the officer who had approached him thanking him and turned to his right jogging over.

Seth was embarrassed that he had jumped the security line unknowingly. What a dunce he thought as he stood next to the barrier and police cruiser.

"Good day sir. Boy did you start a shit storm when you ran out the alleyway. One of our boys down the block caught you running by and called the lobby. Charlie White Capital Police, retired US Army sir at your service."

"Nice to meet you Sargent. Seth Longfield my pleasure, honored to meet you. Call me Seth please."

"Call me Charlie sir. Well, I mean Charlie. So, listen you want to go to the bookstore, McDonald's, Burger King or Starbuck's you let me know. This is my detail Seth, and I am supposed to keep all ya all safe and secure. You gonna run I will have one of my yungin officers run with you or behind you. If you would please allow me that for everyone's betterment. I will catch holy mother of all hades if you do this again."

Seth laughed and asked if they could ride back to the Dubliner together. Seth needed intel and Charlie was his man. "Take me for a drive Charlie, I want to see the immediate area and perimeter around the Dubliner."

Seth wanted to hear Charlie's story. They drove a full circle or perimeter route five times, each loop one block closer to the Dubliner.

"When we get back to the Dubliner pull up just outside

the main entry and drop me off. I want the media to know I am back from a run." White laughed, "YES SIR."

Seth stepped out in full view of the media. He ducked his head in the passenger seat side of the cruiser. "Leave the car hear Charlie and follow me up please."

The entourage of media flicked on their lights and camera's as Seth strode from the cruiser up the small driveway to the main doors of the Dubliner. He nodded to the doorman, stretched his calves against the pillar next to the doorway scanning the media across the avenue and made sure they saw his smile. He would have to navigate that hoard of media bandits that would be waiting to ambush Niles, Elm, Aubrey and Jake. He didn't worry about Jake, however the others would need his shielding from the wolves.

As Seth walked into the lobby two State security people stood at opposite ends of the lobby armed. It was an odd feeling to be back in a secure environment, one emotion Seth regretted and yet embraced willfully.

Sgt. White followed along just one step behind Seth. The newly commissioned Marine's brow was dripping sweat still as Seth approached the head of the security team.

"Seem's, you had a break in security and protocol. Seth Longfield, pleasure to meet you. Sorry I ducked out on you guys this morning. I wasn't thinking about security, I just needed a run. Won't happen again. I asked Sgt. White to be my liaison with the building security, hope you don't mind."

The chief of the detail smiled and said it was not a problem.

"Sgt. Would you please follow me sir." Seth was in command mode now. They entered the elevator and pushed the 8th floor button. It was time for the three S's and then breakfast. He would introduce Charlie to Niles and Jake first.

As the duo exited the elevator Seth turned and spoke to Sgt. Davis.

"You had breakfast yet, I am hungry. I know my godfather is too. Follow me. I want to introduce you to Niles." They entered Seth's room and then he knocked on and open the French Doors to Niles room. The old Salt was already up and had showered. He was sitting in the recliner watching the Outdoor Channel and a fishing show.

"Niles like you to meet Sgt. Charlie White, DC Capital Police. He is the fella charged to keep us all safe. Why don't you two chat some while I shower and dress. Niles, order my four scrambled, order of breakfast sausage, wheat toast, OJ and a bowl of strawberries please. Charlie, you order breakfast too."

"Yes, SIR!"

Check Mate is Coming

Time seemed to slow down for Niles. He was getting antsy. Seth could tell by his look, his demeaner. The discussions of day one on creating a pathway to common ground were sluggish by the lunch break. Chief Elm and Niles had laid out several proposed options and solutions to agreeing the Six Nations some level of oversight on their traditional lands. The United States offered none.

Day one was a day of greetings and conversation until 1500.

Two opposing teams positioning each other, not as collaborators but as defenders thought Seth. Niles asked for a ten-minute break. He needed to speak to Aubrey and Chief Elm.

Seth excused the two old warriors and the true leader

of the Onondaga women, Aubrey. The Clan Mothers of the Onondaga Nation, of all nations across Great Turtle Island were the leaders of the families. The women hold title to all decisions in the end.

Neither team had actually proposed anything of substance to this point. The Six Nations leadership was just listening and asking more questions. Chief Elm offering ideas but no solid proposal. The United States three cabinet members had made no offers of concession on oversight of native lands. The VPOTUS had only made the initial welcoming and comments. Otherwise, he sat nodding his head to Elm's and the other conversations. Seth sensed that something had to change.

It was when Niles, Aubrey and Elm strolled back in the room. Elm smiled at everyone, and Niles winked his left eye at Seth. The old Coastie with the ease of a leopard slowly moved to his place at the table and stood.

"Folk's, Mr. Vice President. I brought this action to amend a wrong, to provide a new beginning to an old agreement. So far, the United States has not offered or proposed any ideas or solutions to the Supreme Court sending this issue of enforcement of the treaty back or should I say, forward to the executive branch. I sued you all, the executive, the congress and the courts. Why?"

Niles stood at his seat looking directly at the VPOTUS.

"I have conferred with Chief Elm, who is the spiritual leader of the Six Nations and also their chief executive. We have agreed to the five actions noted on this yellow pad as the basic foundation for creating a new and emerging collaboration, an inclusive oversight of their traditional ancestral lands. And to the original terms agreed to by President George Washington and conferred by two thirds of the senate long before any of us were born."

Niles passed the yellow pad to Elm, who passed it to Seth, then Aubrey, then Jake and then the Nations lawyer. All four members of the Onondaga Nation delegation nodded in agreement. Seth sat motionless and with the cold stare of a Marine on his post.

Niles walked to his right and took the yellow pad walking around until he was beside the VPOTUS. He smiled and stuck out his hand shaking the Vice Presidents hand.

"Mr. Vice President, sir. Would you please take these five points of action back to the president for his consideration please sir. These are the five values that I and the Onondaga Nation believe provides a collaborative partnering in protecting our shared lands, shared values and the future of the generations yet to come."

Niles was standing tall over the VPOTUS. He might be ninety-six years old, a weakening ticker, this old warrior was offering the Vice President an out he obviously wanted. An exit he needed and desired. Niles tore the one sheet of the yellow pad off and handed it to the Vice President

The Vice President rose, he read the five notations and clasped Niles hand as he smiled and spoke.

"Mr. Gundersen, sir. Your wisdom of age is extremely lacking in our world today. I sense your passion for our nation, it's laws and it's treaties. As I do as well sir. It is my pleasure and duty to take these to the President. For only he can decide and negotiate any amending to the treaty. On behalf of our great nation, thank you for your service to your country as a member of our Coast Guard and former judge. Lt. Colonel Longfield as the Special Master of this proceeding do I have your approval to do so sir?"

Seth stood..

"Yes sir, absolutely sir. That's your call as the leader of the United States delegation, sir."

Seth paused.

"And who sir will be responding to Niles offer. Who will be contacting me to proceed sir?"

"The President will be replying, Lt. Colonel. Thank you all. Mr. Gunderson, Chief Elm, Mrs. Owltree and Chief Owltree I appreciate and am thankful of our meeting today. I learned much more than I ever did in social studies about your true history. I am grateful for that. Now if you please excuse me, I have a meeting with the President."

The US delegation assembled their note pads and excused themselves as Seth and the Onondaga's sat and pondered the moment.

Aubrey spoke first.

"Niles do you play chess, or are you a gambler?"

"Both Aubrey. I prefer chess over poker. It's more of a mind game. Poker is about how deep your pocket is. Why do ask?"

"Well, my father played chess. He loved the game almost as much as he loved Lacrosse. He told me that Lacrosse was a game of the heart and spirit, and that chess was a brain game. Check Niles. Nice move today."

Seth was overwhelmed again by his godfathers wisdom and grace. Always at ease with doing the unexpected.

"Check Mate" thought Seth in his mind smiling.

Running on Empty

The Onondaga Delegation had retired to their rooms. The day's events had been draining of the soul, mind and body for all. Niles had laid down at Seth's insistence. Jake was bored. He needed to be home with his babies and wife.

Seth had called home and spoken to Jakkey. He missed his newborn and her mom too.

Jake knocked on Seth's door.

"Yeah Jake, come on in."

Seth knew the three-knock cadence from their serving together. Like the left eye right eye thing, the knock was between them.

"I am going for a run want to join me. I need to run off some of the boredom and sleezy ooze of DC."

"Give me a minute, also there will be a Marine Sentry joining us. Won't let me run if they don't join us."

"Well, I hope he can run like we do."

"Trust me she can."

Seth called the security team downstairs and said he was going for a run. Seven minutes later a young female Sgt. Major Marine assigned to the team was dressed in a running outfit like any other thirty-two-year-old woman except she had a little side saddle bag that contained her Corp issued handgun and her own little piece of weaponry. A .410-gauge Bond Arms Grizzley. It held two 410 shotgun slugs and could drop a Grizzley at fifteen feet.

The trio entered the freight elevator to the loading dock. As they exited the building a Marine Sentry and his partner saluted Seth and the Sgt. Major. Both saluted back as did Jake.

They were off and running. Two giant men followed by a short athletic female on a late afternoon run.

CNN was the first to see them turn right out of the driveway and head toward the first cross street.

"Follow me guys, I am going to lose these press folks."

Seth broke out into a half sprint. Right then two

blocks, left and two blocks, left again and then head toward the National Mall.

Free of pursuit Seth eased off on the pace. Time to run softly and think. Jake pulled up alongside him.

"What you thinking LTC?"

"About home, getting back to peace and family. How about you?"

"Me too. I miss the quiet peace of the Nation and my family."

They made their way to the wide expanse of the National Mall. The Capital Building to the east and the Washington Monument down west at the far end of the Mall.

Jake took off running like a big old Buffalo.

"Catch me if you can Marines…"

Seth looked at Sgt. Major and said.

"Time to hustle, we'll never catch him."

Jake had good twenty-yard lead as the two stragglers slowly gained pace on the old Marine Indian Chief. Seth and his running partner nearly closed the gap when Jake put on his intense runner pace. The Sgt. Major put it in gear and ran after the big man. Seth slowed his pace and started to laugh gasping for fresh air.

That girl could run, he thought. She closed the gap.

The Indian and the Marine runner pulled up after about one hundred yards both gasping for oxygen. Smiling and laughing.

"You can run with me anytime. Lady, you can stretch it out good."

"Thanks Chief, you have a set of legs there as well. Never seen a six-foot eight man run like a one-year-old buck chasing down a doe."

"You hunt Sgt. Major, you should come visit the Nation if you do. Love to have you as our guest."

By now Seth was walking. Two runs in one day was enough.

The three sat down on a big bench under a shady Washington Oak.

"Sgt. Would you give us a moment please, I need to chat with Chief Owltree."

"Certainly sir."

Jake laughed and stopped her from walking away.

"Sit down Sgt. You have my trust as a Marine and I have the Lt. Colonel's. She earned the right to sit here and chill. Three Marines on a bench. Brothers and sister. What's up?

"You tell me. Niles is leading everything, the VP is useless in this endeavor, not sure what I am supposed

147

to be doing other than sitting and letting the discussion move forward."

Seth cell phone pinged. It showed a restricted call.

"This is Seth, how can I help you?"

"Please hold the line for the President."

Seth rose from the bench and turned looking toward the White House.

"Lt. Colonel, this is the President son. You have a moment to speak?"

"Yes sir, just out for a little run sir. To burn off a little stress and energy."

After a moment Seth said.

"Let me ask sir and get right back to you. Thank you, sir. Yes sir, thank you. And God…"

The line went dead.

"We need to get back and sit with Aubrey, Chief Elm and Niles."

"I got this Lt. Colonel."

She pushed her little handheld button thing.

"I need a car at the Mall for the LTC and guest."

"Double time gentlemen follow me please."

She took off with Seth and Jake jogging along. Both smiling, thinking damn that girl can run.

The Kings Pawn

Once brothers in arms, now brothers in peace. Both Seth and Jake had showered and dressed upon arrival back at the Dubliner in less than five minutes. A Marine style shower was quickly accomplished.

The two towering souls entered the breakfast room Aubrey, Niles and Chief Elm were meeting with Fitzi and Walli. Niles was shaking his finger at Fitzi telling him nope, nope, nope when Seth asked what was going on.

"About to fire my lawyer Seth, son of a guns not worth the damn nickels and dimes I am paying him." Laughing the old Coastie smiled.

Seth and Jake eased into two chairs looking perplexed at one another.

"Fitz tell him what you told Aubrey."

"I told them to have Niles let the President know that the Onondaga Delegation is heading home tomorrow at 0600 if they are not directly negotiating with the executive."

Niles spoke.

"Read the official reply from the White House, son."

Seth read it and handed the document to Jake.

Niles spoke, "I already called downstairs and reserved a rental for you and I to head back to Indian River at 0900. I am leaving too and you're driving unless you want me threading the interstates like Richard Petty running moonshine through the hills of North Carolina."

The room broke out in laughter. Seth laughing and then knowing he would be telling the President the answer, pondering how.

"Well, I need to make a phone call and get my dress uniform on. I need to see the President in person, so he understands the message is delivered. Fitzi, will you get with Mr. Kelly and figure out a way to get me over to the White House without the media or anyone else's knowledge please. I will be back in a flash. Jake, I need your help."

The two peace chief's headed to Seth's suite. Fitzi called

Kelly and they devised a plan for the Dubliner catering van to take Seth to the White House.

"Jake, pull out the blues while I call the White House."

Seth pinged the Office of the President of the United States. He had a direct line to the white house office. This is wild he thought, I am just a publican, and I am calling the leader of the free world.

"Good evening mam, Lt. Colonel Longfield. Thank you. I need to speak to the President please."

Seth was pacing his suite like a tiger in a cage, as Jake laid out the dress uniform of a Marine. Seth had worn the everyday Marine uniform for the meeting that day. Meeting the President required the full dress.

By now Seth was in his skivvies and socks. The President came on the line.

"Lt. Colonel good evening again sir. How can I be of assistance?"

"Sir, I need to see you personally to deliver Niles and the Onondaga Delegations reply to sir. With respect sir this must be one on one with you."

President Lawson was a keenly aware and perceptive

man. His depth of common sense combined with his intellect made him unique among men and the people.

"You had dinner yet son?"

"No sir."

"Well, you're dining with me this evening. Can you be here in thirty minutes. I will send over a car for you."

"Yes sir. However, sir I have a ride…"

"See you soon Lt. Colonel."

Seth dressed with Jake's assistance. In short order the boys repeated the process learned long ago. And then the medals. Seth's breast aglow with his varied medals awarded for his service and sacrifice. As Jake adjusted them, he beamed with pride stepping back. Jake saluted his brotherly soulmate and smiled.

"How's the brass look Jake?"

Jake pinned the brass medal bars on Seth's shoulder strip. He felt a conflicting sense of pride, and spoke.

"You carry the future of our nations Seth in this journey. We shared many a mission as Marines defending this nation, this land of the free and home of the brave. Tell the President the story of Treaty of Lancaster, of Benjamin Franklin recording the words of the great Chief Canassetoga, the Everett Report, tell it all brother.

How my people led your people to freedom, to unification in a confederacy of representatives to form a new nation. How my people fought with your nation for that freedom and that we still do today."

Seth was smiling at Jake with a pride he had never felt before. He put his hand on Jake's shoulder.

"Well, you better get dressed so you can tell him yourself. That's an order Marine."

Arm and arm, the boys walked out of Seth's suite. Seth heading to the meeting room and Jake to his room to put on his Onondaga Dress Uniform.

Guess Who's Coming To Dinner (For the People)

The Dubliner catering van slowly turned left out of the driveway past the media tents and array of camera's. The media were streaming the diversion that Niles had cooked up.

The Onondaga Nation Delegation, Niles and Fitzi stepping out on the large porch above the Dubliner main entrance to get a little fresh air. Fitzi and Dennis Kelly were bookending the group. Fitzi and his cigar. Kelly with a smile so wide it could have been seen on Tipperary Hill in Syracuse, New York.

The van turned right as a Capital Police vehicle pulled out from the curb and took the lead the remainder of the short drive to the White House. The boys were in the rear seat of the Mercedes Van laughing at their escaping notice of this journey. Two Marine Sentry's were seated in the middle seat. Hundreds of times they had begun an adventure together. It was a feeling of warmth and wonderment. Not fear or regret.

Jake began reciting the quick going to battle Thanksgiving Address in his language as Seth followed along. This acknowledgement of what the Earth and Creator provided gave them peace in this moment, and many of those moments of the past.

There was a sense of conflict in Jake's spirit. A Marine and an Onondaga Peace Chief. Two opposing oaths, in one man's allegiance to the people.

As the van slowed the two men saw the gates open following the CPD vehicle. This was unreal for both men. About to meet the Commander and Chief. Both sworn to protect and defend the Constitution of the United States. And they had done so.

The van pulled up to a wide entrance and doorway.

Two Marine sentry's step out of the van first. Then Jake

emerged, the Onondaga Chief in full dress representing the Indigenous People of Turtle Island. The Secret Service and Marine Guards of the White House Protective detail were startled by the six-foot eight man with beads sown on his dress shirt. His headdress was made of deer skin lined with Eagle feathers, Turkey and Owl feathers with two deer horns sown into the array of beauty. Jake was majestic. Regal and proud.

Seth stepped out and every Marine in the detail saluted the newly commissioned Lt. Colonel. Seth standing next to Jake with his hat tucked to his side returned the salute. Then Jake saluted.

"Chief Owltree is with me, gentleman he is a Marine as are we. I believe the President is waiting for us to join him for dinner."

The two giants of masculinity and purpose strode through the door and went through the required screening process all must go through to enter the White House.

Jake was uneasy and Seth felt it.

Jake stopped as they walked and realized he was entering a space he never intended to. He no longer had that tight Marine haircut like Seth. Now his deep dark flowing hair was braided in two tails. His dress shirt was an array of blues, green, and yellow with beads sown in a design his mother had crafted.

Both men were uneasy with the anticipation of dinning with the leader of the free world. The two loving brothers had walked into battle, into dark corners of the world where danger lurks at every bend or doorway. Now the brotherhood was to be tested in ways each knew was unknown.

They entered the outer office of the Presidents executive assistant whose rose as the two giants stood before her. Seth smiled and spoke.

"Lt. Colonel Longfield and Chief Owltree of the Onondaga Nation and the Haudenosaunee Grand Council to see the President."

"Gentlemen if you would follow me, please."

The door opened to the most unique office in America. The Oval Office. President Lawson was standing at the front corner of the large mahogany desk as Seth and Jake entered.

The circle was a spiritually significant symbol in the indigenous cultures of the planet. Nearly every tribe or ensemble of humanity revolved around the circle. The Earth, the Moon, the Sun and the planets revolving around our sun all were circles in life cycle. The Oval Office was a similar space thought Jake.

Just prior to getting to the President's Office Jake stopped, he had to take a leak.

"Excuse me, is there a restroom anywhere I need to hit the head before we meet the President."

The lead Secret Service agent accompanying the duo answered the towering Chief.

"Yes, there is a men's room around the corner on the right."

Seth took the moment as sign to follow his friend.

"Gotta hit the head too."

Jake stood at the sparkling clean urinal on the left and Seth took his spot at the one on the right.

"You nervous LTC?"

Jake stepped to the sink and began washing his hands. Then he touched the eyebrow above his right eye. The next signal was tracing his index finger from the bridge above his nose to the tip. It was one of their personal signals often used in battle or when the two needed secure communication.

After nearly eleven and a half years side by side in

the Marines the brothers had their own code based on touches of normal behavioral motion. Seth would follow Jake's lead keeping an eye on his six, and keep his mouth shut. This was Jake's meeting not his. Seth tugged his left ear lobe, that meant understood and ready.

Bladders empty and the order of command understood the two distinguished souls enter the outer office of the President's Executive Secretary.

Without pause, the door to the Oval Office was opened and Seth stepped in followed by Jake. Seventeen feet four inches of manhood was standing at attention as the President waived the boys in.

"Gentlemen, welcome to The White House. Chief Owltree it is good to meet an America hero and a leader of the Haudenosaunee Nation. Please sit where you feel comfortable."

Seth didn't know if he should salute or stand when the President stuck out his hand to shake Seth's then Jake's hand.

The boys were focused as they glanced around the room looking for exits and doors. Standard operating procedure for these two.

"Mr. President, thank you for seeing me this evening.

I, ah, I. Chief Owltree was helping me pin on my hardware when he started telling me to explain the history of the Treaties from the Two Row Wampum of 1613 to Fort Stanwix and beyond. Well, I figured since he knows the history better than me he should join us for dinner."

The President spoke.

"Son, that is why the Chief Justice recommended you I believe. A good leader listens and lets others speak so they can assess the situation and solutions. I am glad you made that call. Chief the floor is yours sir."

"Mr. President thank you sir, our people, our confederacy of Six Nations once fought great wars against each other. We took captives, burned our enemies villages and life was without peace. Then the Peacemaker showed us the way of harmony, of sharing the Creators bounties amongst each nation. How to form a collective government led by the fifty families of our clans. We buried our weapons under the Peace Tree, a giant white pine on the shore of Onondaga Lake. In doing so we became what was originally five independent nations to form one confederacy. The Mohawk and Oneida to the east, the Cayuga and Seneca to the west with Onondaga as the home of the Grand Council."

Jake stood and walked to the mantle of the fireplace.

"It was the formation of the first democracy in the Western Hemisphere, quite possibly the first of its kind on the planet. That year is known in our lands to be 944 AD. In Onondaga we've kept the fire of democracy burning and the history of our Treaties in our spirit and souls."

Jake paused, looked around and at the picture of George Washington hanging in The Oval Office. He smiled.

"Sir, the history of the Haudenosaunee giving support and counsel to General Washington, Ben Franklin and the other colonists who sought freedom from the British tyranny was documented when our great Chief Canassetoga addressed your leaders on how our nations became so powerful. The year was 1744 in the town of Lancaster, Pennsylvania. A number of the colonial governors met with our delegation to further establish peace and collaboration between you folks and our people. To confirm the Two Row Wampum with a new treaty of understanding. The great chief held one arrow before the assembly and broke it with ease. Then he took a quiver of arrows and attempted to break the bundled arrows. He could not break the arrows when they were together. He was quoted by Benjamin Franklin as saying the following.

"*We are a powerful Confederacy; and, by your observing the same Methods our wise Forefathers have taken, you will acquire fresh Strength and Power; therefore, whatever befals you, never fall out with one another.*"

You have the symbolism on the One Dollar Bill, where our Eagle is clasping them in his talons. In the other talon is the olive branch. The eagle looking down at the olive branch and the 13 arrows showing unity and the power of being one nation. I was a warrior for your nation sir. And I am a Peace Chief from Onondaga and the Haudenosaunee. I come here this evening to establish new and endearing peace amongst our nations here on Turtle Island. One that is based on honoring the Earth, honoring each other and all the Creator brings to those who cherish her gifts."

Jake paused and rose from his chair scratching his right ear. He walked to the glass doors to the walkway outside the Oval. Turning, he smiled. He had given a signal to Seth.

"Mr. President, if I may provide some reference to Chief Owltree's request. My godfather, Mr. Gunderson, brought forth his actions in federal court to establish that the Treaties between our nation and the Haudenosaunee and the other indigenous people whose territories and nations lie with in the United States of America have input and some level of oversight of these shared lands. The Supreme court re-affirmed that the Treaty of Fort Stanwix and others are valid. The Chief Justice made it clear to me that unless there was a reaffirmation of this joint oversight, he would be required to hold the executive branch in contempt."

That last statement was a stretch. The Chief Justice never said that Niles did. He would ask the Supreme Court to hold the Executive Office in contempt.

"Sir, I believe you know the path to coexisting together, to sharing the resources we now understand to be limited. To create a new and endearing model for our nation, for Jake's people and all other nations around this little globe. This is not just about us verses' them or them verses' us. It is really about us verses' us. And sir if "us", being your family and mine have any future it will be understanding and realizing the gifts and wisdom of this continents original residents."

The President rose, he turned to Jake and then Seth.

Slowly nodding his head, he walked back to his desk and open the right drawer. Inside was a small pocket type paperback book. Jake knew the cover well.

"I read this book last night. Someone on my staff suggested I understand what the past leader of the Haudenosaunee wrote down. What he might have been thinking. I love a good book, and this is a book of wisdom. I have read Churchill's writings, Kennedy's, Washington's, Franklin's words, even The Art of War. In my tenure it has been a great experience reading all the words written to page. Their thoughts, the thoughts of the men who sat at this desk with that task of making important decisions can be overwhelming. This little book of some ninety-four pages rivals any of those other books I have been privileged to read and learn from."

The President paused. Then crossed the room to where Jake was standing by the French door to the exterior of the Oval Office. He extended his hand to Jake.

"Chief, you can tell the Tadodaho and Niles that a new treaty will be drawn up to reflect and include the Two Row Wampum Treaty. You have my word and the handshake of the President on that."

Jake was stunned, he seemed to grow from his

six-foot-eight stature to ten feet tall. The President Lawson turned and looked at Seth.

"Lt. Colonel, this is your commission what do you propose as the next steps?"

Seth was not ready for that question. It was one that he had never pondered. He felt uneasy and uncomfortable seated as the two men by door stared down at him. He rose and stood smiling with joyful pride.

"Sir why don't you and Jake sit down and I will detail what I think might work. It has to be some agreement you can take to the Senate for the two thirds vote."

Seth walked over to the President's desk. He was searching for courage, for wisdom. Glancing around the room were paintings of Washington and Lincoln. There were various items of lore and history displayed. And then he saw the map of the fifty United States. He smiled and walked over to the map.

"Sir, we have fifty states, each state has two representatives in the Senate. In Chief Owltree's land there are fifty original families from across five and now six nations. Fifty seems to be a significant number sir. I propose that you, that Jake create a commission of one hundred representatives chosen by each Senator. Each having their own choice. This comes with the caveat that the President signs off on the appointments. I also propose that the indigenous people of each of the fifty states appoint two representatives to the commission. The Tadodaho will have the same oversight as you sir in approving each appointment."

Jake was smiling. Seth was unsettled, he had no clue where or how or what he just proposed came from. It was of the moment, and that was true and genuine.

President Lawson had an intriguing look on his face. Pursing his lips, he looked at Jake. Then slowly he nodded his head again and smiled.

"Chief, what do you think. Sounds like a pretty darn good idea and one that I can sell to the Senate leadership."

Jake shook his head and spoke.

"Yes Mr. President, that is something I can take back to my people and then the other nations. But it is under one condition sir. We must have an equal level of oversight and enforcement of the commission's work in this regard. The future of your people and mine depend on it."

"Who do you think should lead this commission Chief, any recommendations?"

Jake smiled as he put his thumb and right index finger to his chin as if pondering the question. Jake saw the touch and knew he was going to have to find a good manager for the pub.

"Well sir, I believe the Chief Justice of the Supreme Court made that recommendation for you sir."

"Then it seems pretty clear to me. Lt. Colonel. At the end of next week, you will de-commissioned as an active Marine. However, there is one requirement. That you sir, Seth Longfield be the first commissioner of the body."

Seth was cornered. His brother in arms and blood had boxed him in and the President then closed the box.

"Well sir, I ummm, I am honored to be considered. But I am just a dad and barkeep. I have no business leading this mission Mr. President. I mean, the, the responsibility is, is generational sir."

Jake looked at him. At this moment, as a Marine Seth now outranked Jake. However, in the real game Jake still had a little more rank than Seth.

Jake looked at Seth and winked.

"Seth, the President just asked you to serve in this role. It may seem like a request. But as a Marine it seems like an order. The President is asking you to serve, and the only damn answer is, YES SIR."

Seth smiled bowing his head to Jake and then to President Lawson.

"Well, I am not sure how I explain this Betsy, she is already peeved at me for being here these four days. Yes sir, of course I will serve. I get to pick the leadership and we have a deal."

All three men shook hands. It was time for a good meal to seal the deal.

The President led the way to the small dining area directly off the Oval Office. It was a room about forty-five feet by thirty feet with a huge fireplace, large oak dining table adorned with a salad and three pints of Guinness. There were eight beautifully crafted upholstered chairs. They sat down and Jake's phone rang. It was Aubrey. Jake smiled, he smiled whenever his mother called him.

"Excuse me Mr, President. It's my Mom."

He pressed the icon on the iPhone.

"Hi Mom, we have a deal a new treaty…"

Jake paused and Seth could see the color flush out of his face.

"Yes, yes. Okay. You said Reed right. Walter Reed. Yes Mom…"

Jake hung up looking at Seth.

"Niles had a thing. Some sort of heart event. Mom didn't say whether it was a heart attack or just angina. But she called 911. In two minutes, a medic from the Marine guard was attending to Niles. He's on his way to Walter Reed and we have to go."

Jake was in a little moment of shock, of loss. The President moved over and put his hand on Seth's shoulder.

"Come on son, let's get you over to Reed."

President Lawson opened the door and spoke to his lead Secret Service Agent.

"Jim, let's get these boys over the Walter Reed ASAP. We have a family medical emergency. Get the damn beast ready. I am driving them to Reed."

The agent pushed a button on his hand held and barked orders like a Marine Drill Sargent. Sparks were flying and the three men strode down the hall to the awaiting Presidential Motorcade. Forty-five seconds after the Presidents order they were enroute.

Last Breath

It was eight point four miles to Walter Reed. The motorcade covered the distance in eleven minutes and thirty-two seconds. Media alerts went out as the motorcade was enroute. The White House Press Office put out a release.

President Lawson is responding to a medical emergency of someone visiting him this evening and has transported a family member to Walter Reed. The Office of the President will have no further comment on this personal family emergency. There is no health issue with the President or his family. He is just responding to the need for getting the family member to the hospital.

As the motorcade arrived at Reed, Seth opened the door as the "beast" was pulling to a stop. He jumped from the car. President Lawson exited the vehicle after Jake.

There was one lone member of the media onsite. There always was just in case. A pool camera photojournalist. All three major networks, ABC, CBS, and NBC would be live in a moment. CNN and FOX picked up the live feed as America's news networks all brought video to their audience with no real explanation of the issue. The BBC and other international media outlets began coverage. It was the start of media bedlam. Not that the news organization knew what the hell was going on.

Aubrey had ridden in the ambulance with Niles. Chief Elm and Fitzi had been driven over in a Capital Police vehicle. When Elm arrived and exited the photojournalist and media began their speculative assessment of what was going on. And they had no damn clue.

Seth raced into the ER and was escorted immediately to a special ICU only reserved for the President of the United States. The godson was breathless and scared. Niles was all he had left. His mother, father, Archie and his beloved grandmother were all dead. As he walked in Aubrey was clasping Niles' hand and wiping a cool washcloth across his forehead.

"Niles, Seth is here."

Seth moved to the opposite side of the bed that Aubrey

was on. Seth looked at Aubrey, he was weakened by Niles' labored breathing.

"He's been waiting for you. He thinks I am Debbie." Aubrey whispered.

She leaned over Niles and kissed his forehead.

"Niles, Seth is here, say hello."

Niles opened his eyes to see Aubrey and then Seth. He smiled and took in a big breath of air. Niles was connected to every damn monitor there was. The IV was in his left hand. There were beeps and pings and a concert of technology. An oxygen tube was feeding air beneath his nose. He smiled again. In a whispering voice Niles spoke softly.

"Debbie and I have been waiting for you son." Another labored breath. Seth leaned in and spoke.

"Easy Niles, easy. You just rest. You're at Walter Reed Medical and have the best doctors in the world. You have the doctors of the President of the United States making sure you get better. The President's right outside. You did it Niles, we have a treaty."

The former town judge and Coastie gained a little life on that prompt.

"You telling me President Lawson is out there Seth?"

"Yes sir, he drove the damn limo over himself."

Niles took a few sniffs of oxygen through his nose and let a small chuckle out.

"Damn it Seth, invite the man in. You don't leave the leader of the free world standing out in the hallway."

Seth clasped his hand and smiled. Like his grandfather Niles had a level of humor and grace most only wished for. Seth stepped out and invited President Lawson, Elm and Jake into the ICU.

Niles with a surge of adrenaline sat up as the President stepped in.

"At your service Mr. President, Pleasure to meet you."

Niles saluted with his right hand. Lawson exchanged the salute.

The President was unsure of what to do. What in the moment was appropriate?

"Judge, it is my honor to meet you sir. You have one hell of a godson here."

Niles smiled, he clenched down hard on Seth's hand and smiled at Aubrey.

"He will make a good president someday sir."

Niles saluted once more. When he laid back, President Lawson returned the salute.

"I'm coming Peaches, just need to make sure Seth is…"

Niles Levi Gunderson closed his eyes and smiled as one lone tear left the edge of his right eye.

Last Rites

At approximately 2147 the President of the United States ordered all flags on United State buildings and facilities to be lowered to half-staff through Saturday at midnight. His office would be issuing a statement after consultation with the family.

That was all to media was sent.

The President, Jake, and Elm exited the ICU. Only Seth and Aubrey were left with Niles. Seth began to cry. Not just cry but he let all the emotions of losing his father at nine years old, Archie some four years ago and now Niles. The mother in Aubrey began what mothers do when a son is hurting, she hugged him and told the boy of a man that everything would be okay. It's alright to cry and feel grief.

"Seth, Niles loves you and so do I."

The catholic priest assigned to Walter Reed stepped into the room. Niles was a converted catholic.

"In the name of the Father and Son and Holy Ghost…"

Last rites were given. Niles was in Heaven with Debbie.

Epilogue

The Oath of Office

It was a steamy September early morning in Washington, DC. Seth was stretching for his morning run when his phone chirped, he answered. It was 0545.

"Morning Mr. President."

"Morning Seth, how did you know it was me?"

"Who else but you at 0545." The two men were laughing.

"Listen, I know we have dinner planned tomorrow here with the First Lady. What are the Longfield's doing for breakfast today? Why don't you all join us for breakfast. Mrs. Lawson makes great waffles."

Seth looking at the window asked what time. "How's

8:15? I have a few things that I need to discuss with you too. See you then?"

As before, Seth had no time to say yes when the President hung up. He pondered for a moment and then stepped out of the family suite to meet Mara at the staircase before their run.

"The kids and Betsy are still sleeping." Seth whispered under his breath. The duo headed down the steps and out the door. A different security team was on duty. Instead of just the Capital Police there were six suited agents. Seth looked puzzled as Mara stepped over to one of the suits.

"What's up, Staff Sgt. Mara O'Dowd. I am the commissioners security detail. Why the added staffing?"

The agent, Maurice Jennings, showed his ID. Her hunch was correct. United States Secret Service. "We are assigned today to the Longfield family. We'll escort you folks to breakfast with the President this morning." Mara looked at Seth with a wondering glance.

"Yeah, Mara I forgot to tell you. It will be a short run this morning as the President called earlier and Betsy, the kids, and you and I are going to breakfast at 0815." The lead Secret Service Agent asked Mara where they intended to run.

"Down around the Ellipse, I guess. Seth that sound good to you? No more than a fifteen-minute jog I guess. I'm carrying FYI." She showed them her sidearm. Mara turned and off she and Seth jogged slowly. A Capital Police vehicle with two Agents riding along followed the two lone runners.

Mara spoke first.

"Why the extra baggage today. You know something I don't?"

"No, other than we have breakfast at 0815 and our commission committee meeting starting at 1130. What you thinking?"

The Marine attaché with her red hair flowing stepped up her pace. "I don't know, maybe a security threat or something like that. Or they just do this when a big wig is meeting with the President for breakfast. Is dinner still on for tomorrow evening with the First Lady and President Lawson?"

Seth and Mara turned left heading along the west side of the White House and Ellipse. The security team followed. "I guess it's SOP Mara. Let's just run and see if they can keep up." They went into a gallop, double time…

In the fifteen minutes they had been running Mara

and Seth had looped around the Ellipse and were heading back down Pennsylvania Ave. past the Lafayette Statue. The Blair House was in view. When they passed the Marquis de Lafayette Statue the two went to a slow walking pace.

"So I am going to wake the kids and Betsy. Why don't you linger for a moment or two and see if you can grab some intel on the added manpower. Discretely please."

When they reached the Blair House steps Seth waved at Mara as she took in some air. "Gonna wake the kids and Betsy, see you in an hour or so." The doorman opened the door and Seth bounded up the staircase. He was going to shower before waking up his bride. The three S's.

When he was fresh and dressed in the nice blue pants and white dress shirt, Seth kissed Betsy on the cheek. "Wake up princess, we have breakfast at the castle this morning." Betsy rolled over and gave Seth a puzzled look and a kiss.

"Castle, princess. What's up soldier? Treating me awful nice for 0655."

"Well we have breakfast with the Lawson's this morning over at their residence I guess. The President called me at 0545 and asked us to join them. So, get your shower going and I will wake up Jakkey and Gracie. You should probably wear a nice dress or something like that. You can change after breakfast for the trip to the museum with the kids and your Mom."

Seth didn't tell her about the extra detail of six suits assigned and standing outside the front door. Betsy had enough to deal with from this little working vacation. Thankfully her Mother would be arriving today at 10:30 am. Her flight from Detroit was scheduled to land at Reagan. Seth had arranged for the Capital PD to pick her up and bring her to Blair House. He loved when she was around. Betsy would be looking for her text when the jet landed. Gamma, Betsy and the kids were going to do museums and some fun lunches the next here days while Seth toiled away on the work before the commission.

Betsy had picked out two dresses for Seth to give her his approval. A yellow dress with a nice yellow jacket and a blue dress with a cool floral pattern in a watermark style. Seth picked the yellow one. He dressed the kids and put extra diapers in the little backpack for Gracie. She was almost three now, somewhat potty trained but not fully yet. Jakkey was dressed in shorts, a nice button down blue shirt and his Keen hiking boots. He looked the part of a kid from Walloon Lake. When he was told that they would be going to breakfast with the President Jakkey asked Seth if he could wear the little American Flag pin that Seth had pinned to his blue suit coat lapel. Seth helped him pin it to his breast pocket. Jakkey was beaming with joy. Like his dad, wearing red, white and blue.

Seth excused himself and walked down the long hallway to Mara's room and knocked. She let her boss in.

"What's up, what you find out about the added security?"

Mara was dressed in her standard deep navy blue pant suit, a nice pink woman's dress shirt and her navy blue jacket that allowed her to have a weapon hidden. Her sidearm was easily disguised with her shoulder holster, gun on the left side.

"Well, they wouldn't tell me much at all. I didn't probe to deep just general chit chat. But something definitely changed overnight. According to the Cap PD they showed up around 2230 last night. The six we met this morning is the second detail of six. The shift changed at 0400."

"Okay, well lets get everyone together so we can walk over."

Blair House was no more than three football fields from the White House. Seth, Betsy, Mara and the kids walked down the front steps of Blair House. Thankfully, Betsy didn't notice the extra heads on duty. She had her own hands full with Gracie and Jakkey.

When they entered the White House Mara hung back. She didn't like the kids seeing her firearm which she handed over to security. She checked in the weapon and scurried after the Longfield's. Seth was carrying Gracie and Jakkey was holding his mothers hand singing a song from Sponge Bob. He loved Sponge Bob, as every kid did today.

The family entourage was escorted to the private elevator to the Presidential Residence. It had a doorman operating it. When the doors opened to the second floor residence Mrs. Lawson and the President were standing in the foyer smiling. The President leaned over and gave Betsy a little hug and Gracie a kiss on the forehead. She smiled at him. Mrs. Lawson shook Seth's hand and welcomed the Longfield's to their home.

"Jakkey do you like waffles or pancakes?"

"Waffles mam, with lots of Maple Syrup and butter."

President Lawson put his arm around Seth as Jakkey

grabbed Seth's right hand. "Follow me to the Lawson's Waffle House."

The private residence kitchen was unlike most home kitchens. The White House Chef, Jazmine Arnold, was in her second term as the executive chef. She could cook, not just manage a State Dinner. The smell of warm waffles and syrup, the cob smoked bacon from the Lawson's hometown in Virginia, breakfast sausage from a little butcher shop in DC were the main course. The President helped his First Lady get the kids meals plated. Mara and Betsy were handling the herding of the two little jewels.

"Let's fill our plates commissioner and we can enjoy breakfast in my study just around the corner. I have some items we need to discuss." Seth filled his plate with four scrambled eggs, six strips of bacon, two sausage patties, and poured a glass of OJ. Chef Arnold followed the two men with a pitcher of ice water and a big bowl of strawberries and cantaloupe. Lawson loved fruit to top off a breakfast feast. The private Presidential Study was the size of a normal dinning room. The windows facing south toward the National Mall and the Washington Monument.

There was small talk about the commissions work. How long might it take to get an outline of potential collaboration between the US delegation and the representatives from Onondaga, and the other Native Nations? It seemed like a little bit of small talk to have called me at 0545 this morning thought Seth.

"Sir, may I ask you a question?"

"Certainly Seth, that's why we're having breakfast. What questions do you have?"

Seth finished the last of his eggs and was eating his wheat toast with two strips of bacon curled up inside the half slice of buttery delight. He took a big gulp of the cool refreshing ice water.

"I noticed the added man power at the Blair House this morning as Mara and I headed out for our run. Six Secret Service Agents seems a little much for a barkeeper from Northern Michigan. Why the upgrade?"

Damn, this kid was good thought Gerard Lawson. It was why he liked Seth. The man's keen sense of the environment around him, the ability to assess and ask questions. But the thing that the President most admired in Seth was his passion and independence.

Lawson had finished his meal and was sitting back sipping a warm cup of coffee.

"Coffee Seth? You like anything in your coffee son? I

have some Bailey's in the cabinet over there. How bout we touch off our brews with a little dabble of Ireland?'

Lawson pulled the bottle from the cabinet and poured a shot in each coffee mug. "Don't tell the First Lady, she doesn't like me nipping till after five." President Lawson let Seth take his first sip and then handed him over the letter of resignation from the Vice President.

Seth sipped another swirl from the mug, his eyes widening. The Marine felt a sense of sorrow and emotion. He liked the VP, although a politician the guy was sincere and a dedicated leader.

"When did the VP find out he had pancreatic cancer? Jesus, that's just heartbreaking."

"He called me last night. I spoke to him and his wife. We cried and prayed. His senior aide delivered this around 9:30 pm. Truthfully, I was at a loss for about an hour wondering what to do. The guy has been at my side for almost five years. We might not be brothers in arms, but we have built a trust and friendship that I cherish."

President Lawson detailed to Seth that he had made a short list of possible candidates for the fiftieth Vice President of the United States of America. That list was whittled down to three names. He had considered the

Speaker of the House, the Majority Leader of the Senate and two governors. None would truly serve his agenda in the next three years. They would all be running for office, and he did not want that.

"Around 10:15 last night I made my selection. My pick to lead this nation if something unforeseen happened to me. I need someone to carry the banner and help fight for the things the VP and I were tasked with bringing to the American People. I need a partner and someone who has my back."

Seth sensed what that decision might be. The added security team, the agent not answering Mara's questions with any solid reason for the upgrade.

"Sir, may I ask you a question please?"

"Certainly Seth, you can ask me any question any time."

Seth was cornered again by his oath and commitment.

"Seems like you made your decision about the same time as the Secret Service showed up at the Blair House. You're not serious are you Sir?" He paused, clearing his throat slightly and sipping a little ice water.

"You think I am your next VP?"

The President rose and looked out at the Washington Monument and then back to Seth who was standing now.

Shaking his head with a smile the President stuck out his hand to Seth.

"Yes Seth, you're my pick. Like Chief Owltree reminded you a few months back. When the President of the United States requests something from you the only answer is yes. I am asking that you become the 50th Vice President of the glorious United States. I need and the people of America need your leadership, your wisdom and passion to lead this nation forward."

Seth worked his two bear sized hands over his Marine trimmed brow and head. Shaking his head in a little nodding he spoke.

"I serve at your pleasure Mr. President. What's the timetable sir?"

The President detailed the next three hours. He had called the Chief Justice last night and asked that he arrive at the White House by 10:30 am to swear in the next Vice President of the United States. Lawson then told Seth that the current VP's staff would be at Seth command at twelve noon today. The ceremonial swearing in would take place in the Rose Garden at 11:50 am in front of the nation, the media and the world. There would be a private ceremony held at 11:00 am in the Oval Office.

The two leaders then discussed how the Longfield Family would reside at Blair House until after the current Vice President's family moved from the Naval Observatory where the VPOTUS lived, after his passing.

Seth had two major rules that must be adhered to. These were not negotiable. First the family would continue to reside in Walloon Lake in the home Niles had left he and Betsy. Jakkey was enrolled in the Petosky Central School's kindergarten class. He was missing his first few days to be with Seth and Betsy in DC. Second, that if and when Seth was home and wanted to drive to Archies and check in on the business or go hunting or fishing he would be driving himself. The Secret Service can tag along but he was driving his super cab Ford pickup truck when home.

"Well Seth if you are going to do that you need to take the evasive driving course at Langley. We can set that up. The Secret Service is going to have to figure out how to deal with a Marine and barkeep from Northern Michigan. We have a deal, let's go tell the future Second Lady and the kids."

Over the next thirty-minutes Mara watched the kids as the First Lady and the President detailed staffing, housing, transportation, what a Second Lady is expected to do and security. How the Secret Service would always, always be around doing their job of protecting the President and the family of the world's leader. In this case the number two leader.

Betsy asked for a moment to text her mom. "call me when you get in." She explained her mother was arriving for a few days in ten minutes or so. The President chuckled.

"Yes, I know. Seth mentioned that during breakfast. We have a vehicle standing by and two agents at the gate awaiting your mother. Tell her two suits will have a sign that says "MOM" and she should accompany them. You going to tell her where she is headed Betsy?"

"No sir. I think we'll let that be a surprise. I figure I can get a good laugh from her and Seth that will ease my monetary strife with some humor." Seth smiled and winked at her.

When she got the text Betsy let everyone know Gamma was here. She hustled the kids to the washroom for a quick cleaning after breakfast. Thirty minutes later Elizabeth Mahar Longfield, her two children, her mother, Mara, the First Lady, President Lawson and the Chief Justice stood in the Oval Office. Jakkey was sitting on the President's desk holding the *Washington Inaugural Bible*. It was a *King James* version and was the bible many presidents had used to take the oath of office.

Chief Justice Horatio J Jones IV took command.

"Mr. Longfield, if you would raise your right hand and place your left on the bible, please. Now repeat after me."

The pool photojournalist and the White House photographer started recording this historical moment.

> *"I Seth Michael Longfield do solemnly swear that I will support and defend the Constitution of the United States against all enemies, foreign and domestic; that I will bear true faith and allegiance to the same; that I take this obligation freely, without any mental resignation or purpose of evasion; and that I will well and faithfully discharged the duties of the office which I am about to enter: So help me God."*

Seth let the moment engulf him. He smiled and gave Betsy, Jakkey and Gracie a kiss. Then he kissed his mother-in-law. There was one more acknowledgment to be held in private. Vice President Seth Longfield closed his eyes for a moment. He remembered what Niles had said to President Lawson that evening he passed. "He'll make a good president someday sir."

Semper Fi old man, Semper Fi.

© Copyright Dennis S Brogan; The Sustainable Press 2023 / 7GEN Marketing & Branding LLC (All Rights Reserved. May be re-published upon request for use in promotion. Contact thesustainablepress@gmail.com)

Ernest Hemingway's Rules of Writing

1. Keep your first sentence short.
2. Like your first sentence, keep your first paragraph short. You just want to intrigue the reader to read more.
3. Use vigorous language.
4. Be positive.

Number 5 was one he held true. "Never finish your last sentence, that way when you pick it up tomorrow you know where you're going."

About the Author

Dennis Schall Brogan is a business owner, entrepreneur, actor and author. Dennis lives in Syracuse, NY and has spent a career in marketing & advertising working with local, regional and national clients. For nearly thirty years Dennis Schall Brogan has researched the life and writings of Ernest M. Hemingway, and those written about him. The objective was to find Mr. Hemingway's voice. His feelings. In that research and in writing his play about Ernest Hemingway titled, *PAPA An Evening with Ernest*, he began to write in the mornings like Hemingway did. He wrote as a tool for portraying Mr. Hemingway and in doing so fell in love with telling a story and words. Dennis has visited the JFK Hemingway Archives in Boston, the Hemingway Home in Key West and Walloon Lake, Michigan seeking the voice of Ernest Hemingway. Along that journey from the Hemingway Archives at the JFK Museum in Boston to the halls and gardens of his home in Key West, Dennis sought what Hemingway termed the True Gen of that voice. Write one sentence and then write another. Live one moment and then live another.

A Patriot Peacemaker was influenced through Dennis' friendship with Oren Lyons a retired distinguished SUNY Early American History professor. Mr. Lyons is a Native American Faithkeeper and member of the Turtle Clan who resides on the Onondaga Nation. Oren Lyons, is truly one of the planets stewards. During his time working for the City of Syracuse, Dennis became the city liaison to the Onondaga Nation which borders the City of Syracuse. It was during that time he learned of the injustice and neglect of the United States and the treaties with the Haudenosaunee Six Nations.

Dennis is the proud father of Colleen Rose and Meghan Marie Brogan. He is currently writing several other novels. His next work "*Chasing Ernest, A Fish Story*" should be completed by the end of 2023.

Acknowledgements

- Hotel Walloon for providing a beautiful setting for this story to begin.
- Walloon Lake Writers Retreat 2022 for providing those attending the opportunity to explore the art of writing and creativity.
- Dianna Higgs Stampfler for her leadership and coaching authors.
- Thank you to the best storyteller I ever worked with, William Everett Lape. He could warm your heart and chill your soul telling a story.
- Thanks to author Tim Green, a friend and inspiration as a writer. Tim encouraged me and when I asked why he writes, his quote was priceless. "I write because I love the written word, and I love the creative ability that writing provides me."
- Thank You to William & Shirley Brogan for your support and love. A son could not have had better parents.
- Thank you to Paul Kocak who is a great friend and my former high school English teacher. Paul is a great writer! Thanks for your ongoing coffee chats about writing.
- The greatest thanks to "Lord" Kenneth Bowles and his

lovely wife "Lady" Jane Bowles. It was your acting coaching and love of theater that inspired my study of Ernest Hemingway from an actors perspective. That work led to my deep dive research and love of Hemingway. How he wrote, why he wrote, how he loved and how he put pencil to paper.
- Thank you to my third daughter, Cristen Hemingway Jaynes, your hugs and blessings gave me the knowledge that my understanding of Ernest was true and genuine.
- Thank you Matthew Espo for your production wizardry and unending support.

To my sweet daughters Colleen Rose and Meghan Marie, you have made life everything a father could dream of.

Lastly, thank you Ernest for your deep sensitivity and empathy.

Character List

1. Archibald Myers Andersson – Archie Andersson is Seth Longfield's grandfather. Owner of Archies Pub in Pellston, MI.
2. Seth Michael Longfield – Former Marine Pub Owner in Pellston, MI.
3. Niles Gunderson – Archie's best friend and Seth's godfather.
4. Debbie Gunderson – Niles wife and Seth's godmother.
5. Elizabeth "Betsy" Longfield – Seth's wife.
6. John "Jakkey" Ernest Longfield – Seth's son.
7. John "Jake" Owltree – Seth's former Marine buddy and member of the Onondaga Nation located near Syracuse, NY.

8. Aubrey Owltree – Jake's mother and Clan Mother from the Onondaga Nation.
9. Chief Carl Elm – Tadodaho of the Haudenosaunee Six Nations.
10. Alva Andersson – Archie Andersson's wife. Seth's grandmother.
11. Casey – Alva's college friend.
12. Carol Owltree – Jake Owltree's wife.
13. Orlin "Ollie" Owltree – Peace Chief of the Onondaga Nation. Member of the Haudenosaunee Grand Council of Chiefs. Jake Owltree's uncle.
14. Ollie Owltree – Onondaga Nation runner. He is Aubrey's nephew.
15. Jimmy Schall – RV Sales Owner in Northern MI.
16. Edward Owltree – Jake's brother.
17. Antoinette Jackson Owltree – Jake's daughter.
18. Leon Shenandoah – Former Tadodaho of the Haudenosaunee Six Nations.
19. James "Fitzi" Fitzgibbon's – Chicago Lawyer former State Judge in Illinois.

20. Jacobi Durant – Chief of the Odawa Nation in Northern, MI.
21. Devin Lake – Peace Chief of Odawa Nation in Northern, MI.
22. Judge Nolan Dwyer McNally – Senior Judge in the First District of the United States Federal Court, Northern New York.
23. Wallace "Walli" Gibney – Seth and Jake's former Marine buddy who is a constitutional lawyer from Washington, DC.
24. Robert Frederickson – US Attorney in Syracuse, New York
25. Margaret Grace Longfield – Seth and Betsy's daughter.
26. Dennis Kelly – Owner of the Dubliner Hotel and Pub in Washington, DC.
27. Charlie Applegate – Dubliner Limo Driver.
28. Judge Horatio J. Jones IV – Chief Justice of the United States Supreme Court.
29. Judge Caroline Judith Beccerria – Justice of the United States Supreme Court.
30. Shelly Jones – Horatio's wife.

31. President Gerard Foster Lawson – Forty Seventh President of the United States.
32. Mary O'Conner – Vice President O'Toole's Senior Executive Secretary.
33. Sgt. Oscar Davis – USMC.
34. Officer Lt. Charlie White – United States Capital Police.
35. Vice President Alexander Stephen Gardner – Vice President of the United States.
36. Sgt. Major Maureen "Mara" O'Dowd.
37. Bridgette Smyth – President Lawson's Secretary.
38. Jim – Head Secret Service Agent assigned to President Lawson.
39. Jazmine Arnold – White House Chef.
40. Jenny Gunderson.
41. Edward Owltree.

Sources

- The Everett Report- NYS Library; Lula Stillman Papers. Submitted to the NYS Legislature March 17, 1922. https://www.nysl.nysed.gov/msscfa/sc20652.htm
- *"To Become A Human Being: A Message of the Tadodaho Chief Leon Shenandoah;* Leon Shenandoah & Steve Wall, Hampton Roads Publishing March 1, 2002.
- *Two Row Wampum-* 1613, Treaty between the Haudenosaunee and the Dutch. https://www.onondaganation.org/culture/wampum/two-row-wampum-belt-guswenta/
- *Treaty of Lancaster 1744-* Treaty between the British Colonies and the Haudenosaunee, June 30,

1744. http://treatiesportal.unl.edu/earlytreaties/treaty.00003.html
https://www.si.edu/newsdesk/releases/1784-treaty-fort-stanwix-go-view-smithsonians-national-museum-american-indian

- *Treaty of Fort Stanwix-* 1784 National Parks Services; October 22, 1784. https://www.nps.gov/articles/000/treaty-and-land-transaction-of-1784.htm
- *The Nick Adams Stories-* 1972; Charles Scribner Sons New York, New York